"I Have Already Chosen You."

"But that isn't fair! Why does it have to be me?"

His lazy glance took in every curve of her slim body before moving unhurriedly to the lovely face. "Because I wish it," he answered mockingly.

She felt the blood start to course through her veins at his sensuous appraisal and was furious at his ability to inflame her senses even while she was hating him. "You're being completely unreasonable," she raged. "This is just a whim on your part."

His face hardened. "I am used to indulging my whims."

TRACY SINCLAIR
has worked extensively as a photojournalist. She's traveled throughout North America, as well as parts of the Caribbean, South America and Europe.

D1025456

Dear Reader:

I'd like to take this opportunity to thank you for all your support and encouragement of Silhouette Romances.

Many of you write in regularly, telling us what you like best about Silhouette, which authors are your favorites. This is a tremendous help to us as we strive to publish the best contemporary romances possible.

All the romances from Silhouette Books are for you, so enjoy this book and the many stories to come. I hope you'll continue to share your thoughts with us, and invite you to write to us at the address below:

Karen Solem
Editor-in-Chief
Silhouette Books
P.O. Box 769
New York, N.Y. 10019

TRACY SINCLAIR
Flight to Romance

Silhouette *Romance*
Published by Silhouette Books New York
America's Publisher of Contemporary Romance

Other Silhouette Books by Tracy Sinclair

Paradise Island
Holiday in Jamaica
Never Give Your Heart
Mixed Blessing

SILHOUETTE BOOKS, a Simon & Schuster Division of
GULF & WESTERN CORPORATION
1230 Avenue of the Americas, New York, N.Y. 10020

ISBN: 0-671-57174-5

First Silhouette Books printing September, 1982

10 9 8 7 6 5 4 3 2 1

Map by Tony Ferrara

America's Publisher of Contemporary Romance

Printed in the U.S.A.

Flight to
Romance

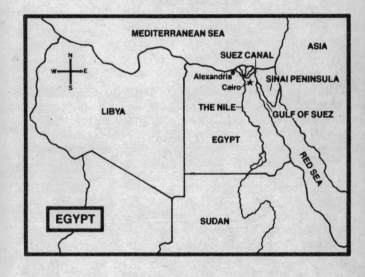

Chapter One

The telephone rang imperiously inside the small apartment, its shrill summons demanding an immediate answer. Jennifer Fairchild juggled her packages precariously and tried to find her door key in the large leather handbag slung over one shoulder. Why do telephones always ring at the wrong time, she wondered? When you're expecting a call, you can wait all day with never a jingle, but when your arms are full and you've had a long day—it never fails!

Finally, her fingers closed over the key ring just as a cardboard egg carton threatened to spill out of her grocery sack. Hastily righting the bag, she opened the door and made a dash for the phone.

"Where have you been? I was about to hang up," Tom Graystock's disembodied voice complained in her ear.

Graystock was her boss at the Visitor's Bureau, the organization responsible for telling the world about the charms of San Francisco and convincing everyone it was the ideal vacation spot. She had just left him less than an hour ago, and after a long day of taking dictation, answering the phone, and being generally useful, she wasn't very happy to hear his voice on the other end of the telephone.

Jennifer set the groceries down gingerly and kicked off her shoes with a sigh. Even an energetic twenty-two-year-old was entitled to be tired after a day like today. She pushed shining blond hair back from a heart-shaped face dominated by wide green eyes, shadowed now by fatigue.

"I had to stop at the market, Mr. Graystock."

"Oh . . . well, I'm glad I caught you anyway." He sounded faintly surprised. Like most men, Graystock had only a vague idea of what it took to run a home. He had never given any thought to the fact that even a single girl who lives alone has to shop and cook. "I have a tremendous favor to ask of you," he said, but his tone of voice indicated that it was more of an order than a request.

"What is it?" She sighed again, knowing ahead of time that it was going to be something she would rather not do.

"We're in a real bind down here. The State Department just called and said that Kalim Al Kahira is arriving at seven thirty tonight at International Airport. He's bringing a whole entourage in his private plane—about twenty or twenty-five people, I believe."

"Who is Kalim Al Kahira?" Jennifer asked, not really interested. The name was vaguely familiar though. Hadn't she heard something about him on the news recently?

"Get with it, Jenny, he's been written up in all the papers—the worldwide charity thing."

"Oh, yes," she said uncertainly, "I guess I did read about him."

His dry tone doubted it. "Well, to refresh your memory, Kahira is head of a group called the Children's Rescue Operation. He founded it, as a matter of fact. It was formed to take care of needy and orphaned children all over the world—the ones who are always caught in the shuffle when another senseless war breaks out."

That struck a chord and she said, "Oh, yes, I've heard of that organization. They do marvelous work."

"Yes. Kahira has been traveling all over the world to sign up as many participating nations as possible, and from what I hear he's been pretty successful."

"He must be a wonderful man," Jennifer commented admiringly.

Graystock's voice was suddenly dry. "Either that or a great politician."

"What do you mean?"

"Kahira is an industrialist with a finger in just about every important pie. Nobody even knows the extent of his holdings or his influence. But public opinion has been turning against these power brokers, so what better way to build a good image than to head up a children's charity?" he asked cynically.

"I think that's terrible!" Jennifer protested. "That's the trouble with people today—they're just too suspicious. How could you even think of such a thing?"

Graystock had the grace to sound slightly embarrassed. "Well, you must admit it's a rather unusual project for a bachelor, isn't it?" he asked defensively.

"Not necessarily, but I didn't even know he was one. I've heard of the work they're doing, but I really don't know anything about Mr. Kahira."

"Then you obviously don't read the gossip columns, Jenny. His name appears regularly, always linked with one beauty or another. None of them has been able to get him to the altar yet, but I don't imagine it's for lack of trying. The guy is a great catch."

"How old is he?" Jennifer asked curiously.

"I think I read somewhere that he's thirty-six."

"That seems awfully young to have built such an empire," she mused.

"Well, I guess he inherited a tidy sum to start with. He comes from one of the most distinguished families in Egypt. But you still have to give him credit. He could have been just another playboy instead of working his tail feathers off like he does."

Now it was Jennifer's turn to be cynical. "It sounds like he manages to combine the two."

"More power to him, I say!"

Ignoring the admiration in her boss's voice, she asked, "What is he doing here?"

"You never know with him, but I gather it's purely a sight-seeing trip. He was in Washington originally, to line up delegates to the first worldwide children's conference that's due to take place in Cairo. After that, Kahira and his party went to New York for a few days to woo the bankers. Everybody thought that would be the end of it but he decided all of a sudden that he wanted to see San Francisco before he went home. Maybe he just wants to relax and somebody told him about the Golden Gate Bridge and the cable cars—you know, all that publicity stuff the Bureau puts out."

Jennifer did indeed know. As secretary to Tom Graystock, part of her duties were to type up "all that publicity stuff."

"So anyway," he continued, "they headed the plane west and he's arriving here in two hours."

Jennifer was puzzled. "I don't understand. What does all this have to do with me?"

"I was coming to that. There are all kinds of high jinks planned for him tomorrow, but the mayor wants the Visitor's Bureau to do the preliminary work and this thing caught us shorthanded. Duggan is out sick, Smith is on vacation, and Paulson is on another assignment and can't get back in time. So it looks like you're elected."

"Elected to do what?" she asked. None of this made any sense so far.

"To take charge of Kalim Al Kahira. Act as liaison."

Jennifer gasped incredulously. "You must be joking! I don't even know what liaison people do."

"There's nothing to know—all the details are being taken care of. They're working frantically right now to clear out a whole floor of the hotel for his party and I've ordered a fleet of limousines to meet them at the airport. We're trying to anticipate his every whim. This is really big stuff for us and I don't intend to goof up."

"It sounds like you've thought of everything," she commented.

"We've sure tried," he answered grimly. "So how long will it take you to get down here?"

"I don't know why you need me if everything's done already." It certainly seemed that the situation was under control and she thought longingly of a hot bath and a bowl of soup with a good book propped up in front of it.

Time was slipping away and Graystock's temper along with it. "I just explained it to you, and if you expect to have a job tomorrow, you'd better get over here right away!" he shouted. "We need someone to greet him and show him around the city and you're it!"

For a minute Jennifer couldn't believe her ears! She thought he merely wanted her to handle the phones in the office. Was he actually suggesting that she play hostess to a prince of finance? "But I wouldn't have the faintest idea what to say to him," she cried in a panic. A thought occurred to her. "Does he speak English?"

"Of course. He was educated at Oxford. All those rich families send their children abroad for their education—their sons, at least. I think he speaks something like four or five languages."

"But *I* don't," Jennifer protested.

"It doesn't matter," Graystock assured her. "All you

have to do is answer his questions about San Francisco. You know—how high is the Golden Gate Bridge and what makes the cable cars go up and down . . ."

"I don't know either one of those answers," she wailed.

"Then find out!" Graystock roared. "From the minute he steps off that plane, you're his official guide. And be sure to treat him with kid gloves. If he wants Chinese food, take him to the best place in Chinatown. If he wants to ride through Golden Gate Park, hire a carriage. Expense is no object—just give him what he asks for. That's what he's used to."

"But Mr. Graystock . . ."

He interrupted her impatiently. "I don't have time to argue with you. Be here in fifteen minutes."

Jennifer heard the emphatic click that disconnected them and she stared at the phone for an unbelieving moment. Her job had always been pleasant enough, although not very stimulating. In spite of the agreeable working conditions, there was no real future at the Bureau and she might have gotten restless except for the bright prospects in her future.

During the summer, Jennifer had done extensive volunteer work for the congressman from her district and in the process gotten to know him well. His chances for reelection in November were bright and he had practically promised her a job on his staff. The idea was heady stuff and she had her fingers crossed. Tom Graystock knew about the opportunity and was all for it.

"This is no place for you, Jenny." He was the only one who ever called her that. "Nothing ever happens around here."

That had been her feeling too, but it seemed they were both wrong. Who would ever have believed that from a routine job as a secretary she would suddenly be asked to mingle with the jet set?

Well, not exactly, she chided. Jennifer had always considered herself level headed and there was no sense getting panicky about this thing or painting a romantic picture either. So what if he was a millionaire industrialist? When you came right down to it, she was just going to be a tour guide like one of those ladies who took people around the museum. All she had to do was make a short welcoming speech and ask him how he would like to spend the evening.

What would he be like? Spoiled of course. Just look at all the commotion he was stirring up before he even got here. But what did he look like? She had forgotten to ask, but Jennifer was almost certain he would turn out to be short and fat. The fact that he was noted for his beautiful girl friends didn't mean a thing. There were always women willing to flock around that kind of money!

But this was no time for conjecture. The minutes were flying and decisions had to be made. First of all, what to wear? Shuffling rapidly through the closet, she considered and discarded several choices. The trouble was, her wardrobe wasn't geared to high society. Mostly it ran to skirts and blouses and sweaters. The only suitable dress was a soft yellow silk, but was it too daring? The halter neck plunged dangerously low in front and left her back bare almost to the waist.

She had bought it on sale and the price had been terribly steep, even marked way down. At the time, she had had no place to wear it, but she couldn't resist its silken luxury.

Smoothing the elegant fabric over her slender figure, Jennifer eyed herself with satisfaction and felt justified in skipping all those lunches to pay for what had seemed a terrible extravagance at the time.

With one eye on the clock, she jumbled the essentials into a small evening bag and caught up a white wool coat. Taking a last look in the mirror, Jennifer sighed.

Wouldn't it be nice to have a fancy fur wrap to go with the dress? She made a face at herself. Wasn't it enough that her date was practically a prince? Even Cinderella hadn't asked for a fur coat! Laughing at her own nonsense, she ran lightly down the stairs.

Graystock was pacing up and down the office like a caged lion even though she had almost set a record getting there. "It's about time! What took you so long?"

Jennifer was breathless. "I hurried as fast as I could."

"Well, you're here now—that's all that matters," he said, rather ungratefully, she thought, considering how she had rushed. "Come on, I'll walk you downstairs."

Now that the moment was actually at hand, all her doubts rushed back. "I still don't understand why you can't go yourself."

Her usually calm boss gritted his teeth. "All right, I'll change places with you. Do you feel capable of handling the calls from Washington, checking on the hotel, hiring men to—"

"Okay, I get the message," she interrupted. "I'm just so afraid I'll let you down." A terrible thought suddenly struck her. "How will I know him? He won't have any idea who to look for and suppose I miss him at the airport?"

"Don't worry. Private planes don't land where the commercial jets do. The chauffeur of your limousine knows where to go. When the plane comes in, you'll spot it. For one thing, there will be police swarming all over the place."

"But how will I recognize him?"

"Well, let's see—I saw him on television. He has dark hair and he's tall."

For what it was worth, there went half of her preconceived notion. "That's no help," Jennifer protested. "That description could fit most of the men in his party."

"Then *ask* somebody! I don't know now you're going to find him. Just find him!" Graystock exploded, and she realized that he was feeling the pressure too. It didn't add to her peace of mind. What kind of man was this who had everyone scurrying around like a flock of frightened starlings?

He was probably detestable—rich, spoiled, and utterly impossible. And she was responsible for entertaining him. Jennifer shivered at the thought. He would surely expect to be greeted by a movie star at the very least, and what was he getting?—Jennifer Fairchild, secretary and general flunky.

She would be at a disadvantage from the beginning. Would he at least be civil or would he come right out with his displeasure? It was no comfort to realize that he could do it in a choice of four or five languages.

In all too short a time the car arrived at the airport, but instead of going to the main terminal, it turned left down a long dark road leading to a fenced-off area. The driver seemed to know where he was going and proceeded to a gate attended by a uniformed guard. After the two men exchanged a few words, the gate opened, and they drove right onto the field where a long sleek jet airplane had just landed. Mr. Graystock was vindicated for rushing her so mercilessly. It seemed Jennifer had arrived just in time.

As soon as the heavy door of the plane swung out and sideways, a swarm of men emerged. Most of them were young and they were all dressed in the conservative garb of the businessman—dark suit, white shirt, and tie. Looking at them, Jennifer's heart sank. How would she ever pick her quarry out of the group? But her fears were groundless.

After everyone else had bustled out there was a pause, and then a man appeared in the doorway. As he stood on the top step, she knew immediately that this was Kalim Al Kahira.

He was the only one dressed casually, but that wasn't the clue. It was a magnetic aura that set him apart from all the others, a leadership quality that was unmistakable. Waiting at the head of the stairs and surveying the field as though he owned it, he was the focal point of the scene—the cause of all the commotion but completely aloof from it. As he turned slightly, the moon silhouetted his strong profile, outlining the aquiline nose and firm chiseled lips.

Jennifer caught her breath, unaware that she was staring like an impressionable teenager. In the cold starlight there was something cruel and hawklike about his face. It conjured up wild rides across a windswept desert astride a beautiful Arabian stallion. This was no pudgy, lethargic little businessman. This was a captain of industry, a man of action! He was the fabric of every girl's dreams—rich, handsome, powerful—and utterly unattainable.

She stood at the edge of the crowd, gazing at him with shining eyes and parted lips, oblivious to the activity swirling around her. Busy men unloaded mounds of luggage and called to each other over the din. But the center of attraction was the top of the stairs where Kalim Al Kahira stood, and she knew intuitively that it would be true no matter where he was.

Becoming increasingly impatient with the endless delays of arrival, his glance started to wander over the crowd. Suddenly he noticed her standing alone and their eyes met. Jennifer started to tremble. It was one thing to stare appreciatively at an idol. It was quite another thing to have it come to life and stare back at you!

After a few low words, the men surrounding him moved aside, making a path for him to descend, and he walked slowly and deliberately toward Jennifer, whose heartbeat quickened. Nothing had prepared her for a man as devastating as this. What could she possibly say to him?

When he reached her side, she had to tilt her head to look up at him and her tension increased. From a distance, she hadn't realized how tall he was, or just how devastatingly masculine. Seen at the top of the stairs, he was a remote godlike figure. But at close quarters, he was all too human. Broad shoulders tapered to slim hips, and as he towered over her Jennifer wondered irrationally what that firm mouth would feel like against her own.

A quiver of emotion swept over her at the idea and was instantly replaced by shock. What on earth had gotten into her? She had met a lot of handsome men, but such a thought had never occurred to her before.

Fortunately, he didn't know about her momentary aberration! Or did he? The expressionless black eyes that subjected her to a thorough inspection gave nothing away and she squirmed with embarrassment. Finally, he spoke.

"You have come to meet me?" His voice was low and sensual, the English letter perfect but with a musical foreign accent.

Jennifer nodded her head dumbly, incapable of speech. Part of her mind registered the fact that his navy sport coat was undoubtedly cashmere and the creamy shirt he wore with it the finest silk. She was staring with bemused fascination at the matching ascot knotted carelessly around his bronze throat when he spoke again, this time with a touch of impatience.

"Do you have a car? I would appreciate going to the hotel now. We have had a long journey."

Jennifer turned hot and cold all over. She was behaving like an idiot, and if Mr. Graystock ever found out, he wouldn't just fire her, he would skin her alive. "Oh, I'm . . . I'm terribly sorry. The car is right over there." She gestured toward it. "Won't you get in? And . . . and . . . I mean, if there is anyplace special you want to go, well . . . I mean, I'm here to do anything you want." Good heavens, what a dumb greeting! That wasn't what she had rehearsed.

An enigmatic look passed over his face, but he merely said, "The hotel will be fine for now."

"Yes sir. You bet," she said inanely, and led the way to the waiting limousine.

Amid a general flurry of activity, all of the party found places in the long line of cars drawn up for the purpose and Jennifer and her charge entered the lead car. But before the chauffeur closed the doors, one of the men from Kahira's party slipped into the front seat next to the driver.

He was a veritable giant, as tall as Kahira but built like a wrestler. Huge biceps strained the material of his dark suit and Jennifer had the feeling that he was uncomfortable in Western attire. Thick eyebrows that almost met over black eyes opaque as marbles made his face look formidable, while an ugly scar curving from just above his left ear to the edge of his jaw added to the general feeling of menace.

With some trepidation, Jennifer leaned forward to tell him that this car was reserved, but before she could explain, Kahira tapped her on the shoulder.

"It is all right," he said. "Habeeb goes everywhere with me." He spoke a few unintelligible words to the man, who looked at her with no change of expression and nodded his head.

Didn't he speak English? Jennifer shrugged. It was just as well—this way she needn't have any conversation with him, which was all to the good. He was scary-looking. She turned her attention to the man she had come to meet.

"I should have introduced myself sooner, Mr. Kahira. My name is Jennifer Fairchild and I was sent by the Visitor's Bureau. We would like to welcome you to our city. I've been assigned to show you around San Francisco. Is there anything special you would like to see?''

He smiled and the effect was devastating. Even white teeth showed in his tanned face and the intense dark eyes sparkled, making him seem infinitely more approachable. "I have never been fortunate enough to visit your lovely city before, but I have heard much about it. I wish to see it all before I leave.''

Jennifer felt slightly overwhelmed, but she answered gamely, "I am sure that can be arranged.''

"You will please tell me about the points of interest.''

Jennifer gulped. This was what she had been dreading. Why on earth hadn't she paid more attention to all those press releases giving facts and figures?

"Well, San Francisco, like Rome, is built on many hills—some of them so steep that the sidewalks have steps for pedestrians. Otherwise, they might slide right down to the bottom." This was usually good for a smile, but when he merely regarded her with polite interest, she plunged on. "We're noted for our Fisherman's Wharf and Ghirardelli Square, which used to be a chocolate factory. Also for Golden Gate Park, which covers many miles and houses live buffalos, museums, and an authentic Japanese tea garden, among other things.''

As the big car made its way toward the city, she dredged up all the information she could think of but with growing apprehension. For some time her illustrious guest had not really been paying attention to the travelogue and Jennifer was terribly afraid that she was boring him.

He had become increasingly withdrawn and now, turning a penetrating gaze on her, he asked suddenly, "Are you paid to do this?''

For a moment she was nonplussed—what a strange

thing to ask! Why on earth would he want to know that? "Well, yes, it's part of my job," she answered. This was no time to worry about a small lie and actually it really was her job tonight. "The Bureau always provides an escort for VIPs, which means Very Important Persons, as you know. I'm here to see that your visit gets off to a pleasurable start."

His mouth curved in a cynical smile. "I believe I understand. It seems to be a universal custom, but I wanted to be sure."

He looked at her appraisingly and Jennifer felt distinctly uncomfortable. It was a decidedly male look that lingered overly long on the soft curves displayed by her plunging neckline, imperfectly covered by the wool coat, which had fallen open.

She resisted the urge to pull it together, assuring herself that she was being ridiculous. He certainly couldn't be interested in *her* and they were well chaperoned by the chauffeur and that thug, Habeeb, although he was small comfort.

To cover her nervousness, she said, "After you're settled in the hotel, would you care to see something of our city?"

His eyes bored into hers. "Is that the custom?"

"Well, most people want to see the Golden Gate Bridge and Chinatown. They're quite famous. But if you're too tired . . ." Her voice trailed off. Would Mr. Graystock blame her if he refused to go sight-seeing?

"No, that would be fine. I will refresh myself and then we will go to see your bridge."

"I think you will find it quite beautiful," she said, "but perhaps you would like to have something to eat first?"

"An adequate meal was served on the airplane. We will go first to see the city and then you will come back to my apartments and I will order a late supper."

Before she could answer, they pulled up in front of the hotel, and once more bedlam reigned. Twenty-two people and what looked like a mountain of luggage can create a traffic problem in the most well-regulated hotel.

Jennifer stood prudently on the fringes while scores of bellmen and all the hotel's top brass catered to the illustrious party. Curious tourists gaped while suitcases were loaded on carts and the necessary amount of elevators were commandeered to lift the newcomers directly to their floors with no stops in between.

Kahira looked around, annoyed by even the slight delay, and, spotting Jennifer standing unobtrusively by a giant marble pillar, beckoned impatiently. "Come, come!"

"I'll wait down here for you," she said.

He looked faintly surprised and started to say something, then changed his mind. After he disappeared into a waiting elevator, Jennifer sank down gratefully on a velvet banquette. She was overwhelmed by all the fuss and ceremony occasioned by this high-level visit and it was good to be alone for a few moments and collect her thoughts.

This whole experience was mind boggling! The world of Kalim Al Kahira was completely outside her ken. What would it be like to be that rich, she wondered?— to be able to book a whole floor at the Mark Hopkins. It was hard even to imagine.

She had been taken to dinner once at the Top of the Mark, the beautiful restaurant overlooking the whole city. It had been her birthday and a visiting uncle had splurged on a lovely and unexpected party for her.

Jennifer would never forget that evening. All the tables had flowers adorning snowy tablecloths and a platoon of attentive waiters served delicacies and even a small birthday cake decorated with a sparkler. The

21

fizzing sparks were reflected in the broad expanse of glass windows, rivaling for a brief moment the millions of lights glittering below.

It was an unforgettable experience for her, but if you were a tycoon you just took that sort of thing for granted. Kalim Al Kahira could dine there every night if he liked. Wealthy people did what they wanted and didn't even think of the cost.

She smoothed the skirt of the lovely yellow gown and thought, If I were that rich, I wouldn't have needed to wait till this dress was on sale. I could have ordered it in every color. But, on the other hand, did you appreciate things as much if you didn't have to work for them? Lost in the academic question of whether there were any benefits that accrued to the poor, Jennifer didn't realize that her charge was standing in front of her.

Startled out of her reverie, she said, "Oh, Mr. Kahira, I didn't see you."

"Suppose you call me Kalim," he said, a tiny smile touching the corners of his sculptured mouth. It changed his expression and in that moment Jennifer saw the charm that had devastated so many women. It wasn't his money or his power. Without a cent to his name, this man would have women besieging him.

She looked into his dark eyes and her heart did a funny little flip. A couple of hours ago, she hadn't even known he existed, and soon he would be gone as suddenly as he had entered her life. But she had an uneasy feeling that he would leave his mark.

"Shall we go?" he asked.

The touch of his hand on her elbow was like an electric current running through her body, but she knew it was only caused by an attack of nerves. Rising to her feet, she followed him out to the waiting limousine.

In the confines of the closed car Jennifer was more

than ever aware of the sheer masculinity emanating from this man. His broad shoulders lounged casually against the plush upholstery and his long legs were stretched out comfortably, in direct contrast to her tense body perched primly on the edge of the seat.

He was regarding her with a raised eyebrow, a definitely questioning look on his face, and her heart started to thud until she realized that he was only waiting for her to give the driver directions.

Following her hasty instructions, the chauffeur wheeled the big car down California Street to Chinatown, a short block away.

"I think it would be better if you sat back," Kalim told her, and she detected a glint of amusement in his eyes. "If the driver made a sudden stop, you might be injured."

His words were polite but Jennifer knew that he was laughing at her. Did her insecurity show that much? She was grateful that they had such a short distance to travel.

As soon as their limousine made a left turn into Chinatown, he turned his attention to the exotic sights, much to her relief. The brilliantly lit stores had Chinese characters written on the fascia boards and even the telephone booths had a Far East flavor. Each was a miniature pagoda painted in bright colors. The streets were thronged with Chinese and many of the older people wore the traditional garments of their native land.

Suddenly Kalim leaned forward. "Stop here," he commanded. "We will walk for a time."

He took her elbow in a firm grip, and while the long black car crawled along beside them through the narrow street, they strolled past shops exhibiting colorful silks, Oriental souvenirs, and strange, unidentifiable foods.

Kalim paused in front of a shop that had a small abacus in the window, a wooden frame with little beads strung on wires. "Ah, I must have one of those. It is a Chinese adding machine. Amazing the way they use those to tote up sums. I have seen them do it."

They entered the store like two ordinary tourists, and in addition to the abacus Kalim bought two beautifully dressed dolls with silken black hair and richly brocaded robes.

"These will make nice gifts for certain ones at home," he said with satisfaction.

Two dolls? Jennifer thought. Well, what did she expect? That was probably only the beginning. He undoubtedly had a whole list of girls to buy for. That's the way playboys live, she told herself. It certainly doesn't matter to me. He will be gone in a day or two and I'll never see him again, so what difference does it make? But the little nagging feeling of loss surprised her.

Farther down the street they came to a lovely jewelry store and Kalim said, "This is what I have been looking for. Come, we shall go in."

Obediently, she followed him inside. Kalim had good taste—this was no ordinary tourist shop. It was filled with precious and unusual items. Together they looked at strands of glowing jade—not only green, but lavender and black and even a deep shade of red.

"Do you mean that all of these are jade?" Jennifer asked incredulously, feeling like a visitor in her own town. "I thought jade was always green."

"Oh, no, miss." The old Chinese man behind the counter smiled and shook his head. The embroidered satin coat he wore was as colorful as the jewels he offered for sale and it was obvious that he had a special feeling for beauty. "There are many varieties. Even the greens are different in their own way. Here we have the lovely clear apple green." He handed her an exquisite bracelet. "And here is the glowing emerald and the deep leaf green." The glass counter soon became heaped with treasures as he withdrew them lovingly to show her.

"This one matches your eyes," Kalim commented, indicating a ring. "Which one do you like?"

"They're all so heavenly it would be hard to choose," Jennifer said, "but I think I like this one the best. Isn't it gorgeous?" She pointed to a delicate lavender pendant, not the most lavish but intricately carved and hanging from a thin gold chain.

Kalim clasped it around her neck and Jennifer's spine tingled at the touch of his long fingers on her bare skin. He stood back, regarding her with satisfaction, and she felt herself flush as his dark eyes swept down the deep neckline of her dress.

"We will take it," he told the old Chinese man.

"Oh, but I think you should make your own choice," Jennifer protested. "You know better than I what she would like. The person you're giving it to, I mean," she explained, suddenly uncomfortable. It was one thing to know he was buying for a whole flock of playmates. It was another thing to put it into words.

"You said it pleased you."

"Well, yes, *I* like it, but . . ."

"Then that is all that matters. It is for you."

"For me?" She was aghast! Good grief, he didn't think she was hinting did he? "Oh, no, I couldn't possibly take it, Mr. Kahira."

"Kalim, remember? And of course you can take it."

"No, it's completely out of the question," she assured him.

His brows drew together. "It is my gift to you. You would insult me by refusing." And indeed, he did seem insulted. His mouth was a straight line in his arrogant

25

face. "It is the custom of my country. We are used to paying for what we receive."

Jennifer wished he hadn't put it in quite that way, but she realized that, although he spoke perfect English, there were limits to his understanding of the nuances of a foreign language. Foreign to him, anyway. Also, it made her quite nervous when he became imperious.

There was something very chilling about those narrowed eyes and Jennifer was reminded of the tremendous power he must wield in his own country. The male-female relationship was different there, too. Eastern women weren't as outspoken as American girls. In spite of the strides they'd made, it was doubtful if they ever said an outright no to anything.

"I'm sorry. I didn't mean to appear ungracious," she apologized. "It's just that it's such a magnificent gift that I'm quite overwhelmed."

There didn't seem to be any graceful way to refuse, although Jennifer couldn't help wondering what Mr. Graystock would say if he knew.

"It's . . . it's very lovely. Thank you so much," she said, fingering the pendant nervously. He appeared mollified, so she quickly added, "And now perhaps you'd like to get back in the car and we'll do a little tour of the city." Best to get him away from the shops speedily!

As they drove around, Jennifer pointed out the various points of interest, but Kalim paid scant attention. Sight-seeing was relegated to the background and he now seemed much more interested in her. His dark eyes held banked fires as they took in every curve of her body, and Jennifer's nerves tensed, although he made no move toward her.

"You are not married." It was more of a statement than a question. When she shook her head, he asked, "Do your parents know how you make your living?"

"My father is dead and my mother is in a sanitarium

in Colorado," she answered, "but yes, she knows I work for the Visitor's Bureau."

He considered this with raised eyebrows. "Do you live alone?"

"Yes, I have my own apartment. It's tiny, but you wouldn't believe the rents in this city!" As soon as the words were out of her mouth, Jennifer felt foolish. Why had she mentioned that? Kalim wouldn't have any conception of what it was like to live on a budget!

But he was nodding his head. "Ah . . . I understand. That is why you must provide your services—to exist."

"Well, I wouldn't exactly . . . I mean . . ." Oh, dear, it was hopeless to explain that he was being quite insulting. She sighed and said, "I have to work for a living—let's put it that way."

"Are there many girls like you in this city?"

Jennifer laughed. "Yes, there are thousands of us."

"So many?" He appeared thoughtful.

Glancing out the window, she saw that they were nearing the Golden Gate Bridge, and she leaned forward and said to the driver, "Pull up here for a moment please." And then, to Kalim: "There it is—the pride and joy of San Francisco."

The bridge was at its best in the cool crisp moonlight. Bedecked with lights like sparkling chains of canary diamonds, it guarded the approach to the city. As they watched, the headlights on rows of cars moving in both directions formed brilliant hyphenated lines.

"It is indeed a sight to behold," he said.

The stars formed a canopy over the bridge and they sat silent in the darkened car, awed by the magic wrought by man and nature working in harmony.

Finally Kalim broke the silence. "Now we will return to the hotel."

Jennifer's emotions were mixed as she realized that her date was almost over. In many ways it had been a trying evening, but worth every uncertain moment.

She had never met a man like Kalim before and she had a feeling she never would again.

During the short ride back to the hotel, she gamely tried to point out additional landmarks, but Kalim barely glanced out the window. He spent the time inspecting her minutely with an appraising glance that made her tremble. There was no doubt that he was seeing her as a woman and the closed car provided an uncomfortable feeling of intimacy.

The thought crossed her mind that it was fortunate they were in her country and not his. In spite of his sophistication, there was something pagan about this man. On his own turf, Jennifer imagined, he would probably be sweeping her up in his arms and carrying her off to some walled palace with tinkling mosaic fountains and soft couches scattered with velvet cushions.

It was a ridiculous thought. Kalim was a civilized man, not some lascivious sultan! But a pulse started to beat in her throat and she covered it with one slim hand, afraid that he might notice. Her gesture had the opposite result she had intended as Kalim's attention was drawn to the slender curve of her neck, where a pale tendril of hair curled forward. As he leaned toward her to brush it away, the car pulled up in front of the hotel.

She was relieved yet curiously disappointed. Her cool skin tingled from a touch that was feather light but still managed to be intimate. There she went imagining things again! Jennifer was disgusted with herself for being so unsophisticated. His simple gesture hadn't meant a thing, nor did she want it to. There was nothing personal in this whole evening. It was strictly business and it was time she realized it.

Pinning a bright smile on her face, she said, "Here we are, Mr. Kahira—I mean, Kalim. I hope you enjoyed the evening." Why did she suddenly feel like an awkward schoolgirl? Struggling for poise, she extended her hand most formally. "It's been a great pleasure meeting you."

He frowned at her. "You will come up to my apartments. I have ordered supper."

It suddenly occurred to Jennifer that she hadn't had anything to eat since lunch while he had mentioned dining on the plane. Since she was convinced that he was only being polite, she said, "It's really quite late and I'm sure you're tired. Perhaps we should skip supper."

But he took her arm impatiently and propelled her into the lobby. "You are right, it is quite late. Let us go up at once."

Jennifer was completely nonplussed. If he agreed that it was getting late, then why was he insisting that she join him in supper? Did he feel that he owed it to her because she had shown him around? Whatever the reason, his firm grip brooked no argument and she followed him without further protest.

Kalim's hotel suite was the ultimate in luxury. The sitting room was furnished with deep couches and there were huge bouquets of flowers scenting the air. Heavy drapes framed tall picture windows overlooking the city and a profusion of lamps cast a rosy glow on a table beautifully set for two. The white linen tablecloth displayed delicate china and silver instead of the standard hotel ware.

As she was admiring the room, Habeeb came out of a door on the left and bowed to Kalim, touching his chest, his throat, and then his forehead. He completely ignored Jennifer and she reflected that either women weren't very important in his part of the world or he didn't like her personally.

The two men exchanged a few words in their native

tongue and then Habeeb left. She was relieved when the huge man glided from the room. There was something about him that gave her the creeps.

"Is Habeeb your valet or bodyguard or what?" she asked.

"He is totally devoted to me," Kalim said, not quite answering her question. "He would kill for me."

Jennifer looked to see if he was joking, but he seemed completely serious. "Isn't that a little extreme?"

"It is a matter of loyalty. His main concern is my welfare and he would move heaven and earth to insure my happiness and the well-being of anyone close to me."

As Kalim spoke, he walked slowly toward her, and Jennifer felt suddenly vulnerable. He seemed aware of it and a mocking smile curved his lips as he towered over her, totally masculine and in control of the situation. A small finger of fear touched her spine. But that was ridiculous, wasn't it? They were here in San Francisco, not in some seraglio in the Middle East.

His eyes were dark and impenetrable as he asked, "Would you care to eat now or later?" She looked at him uncertainly. It was so hard to know what he preferred and she didn't want to make a mistake at the very end of the evening. Sensing her indecision, he said, "Perhaps you would care for a glass of wine first."

She nodded, grateful that the decision had been taken out of her hands, and Kalim went to the silver wine cooler, where a bottle of champagne was chilling. Jennifer breathed a small sigh of relief. She was ashamed of being so nervous but Kalim had that effect on her. It was hard to think when he was close. Although he had acted the perfect gentleman all evening, there was a feeling of leashed passion about him that made her light-headed. Turning toward the tall windows to compose herself, Jennifer heard a cork pop, signaling that the wine was opened.

He came up behind her as she was looking out at the spectacular view and she turned quickly—too quickly. He was standing so close that their bodies touched as she faced him and his arms went around her, drawing her against his hard length.

Instinctively, Jennifer tensed and tried to pull away, but his arms were unyielding, refusing to release their captive. This was what she had feared, but when she looked up to protest, his mouth covered hers possessively. Apprehension alerted every nerve when Jennifer found she was powerless against his dominant strength, but his kiss wasn't the punishing, passionate one she expected. Instead it was slow, almost lazy, an unhurried exploration of her lips. She struggled briefly, but he could tell that her treacherous body was responding to his light caresses.

At first she was like a startled doe caught in a steel trap, but her panic subsided under repeated kisses that were gentle enough not to frighten her. And when they grew more demanding, it was too late. He knew exactly how to arouse her every sense, and although Jennifer dimly recognized the danger, she was already drawn into a vortex of tumultuous feeling that drained all will to resist.

One hand caressed her neck and a questing forefinger teased its way down her bare back, while his warm mouth slid over her cheek. She trembled under his expert touch and wildfire coursed through her as his tongue tasted the creamy skin of her earlobe. Clutching his shoulders with helpless hands, she closed her eyes and gave in to the waves of emotion washing over her. Her kindled body relaxed willingly against his, ignoring the warning that her brain tried to sound.

When his mouth returned to hers, she welcomed it

with a soft sigh of ecstasy and her lips parted eagerly under the increasing urgency of his. Light kisses were pressed on her eyelids and the vulnerable spot behind her ear, but always his mouth returned to reward her own.

It was like a dream of heaven until Kalim's hand moved inside the plunging neckline to curl around her breast, his thumb moving in a sensuous circle over the coral point. A shudder of fierce desire wracked her even as the dream fragmented, and Jennifer realized she had to fight not only him but herself as well.

Putting her hands against his chest, she dragged her mouth away from his. "Kalim, you mustn't . . ."

But he interrupted, his voice harsh and autocratic. "Be quiet! The time for talking is past."

Lifting her effortlessly in his arms, he carried her toward the bedroom and the spell was finally broken. The shock of his intentions brought Jennifer to her senses and she started to struggle in earnest, beating against his hard chest with small, ineffectual fists.

"Put me down! What do you think you're doing?"

He looked at her uncomprehendingly. "What kind of nonsense is this?"

"That's what I'd like to know!" She wriggled out of his arms and faced him furiously. "What makes you think that every girl you meet is going to fall into bed with you?" It didn't help to realize that she must have given that very impression herself.

His face was a study in conflicting emotions. "Why else are you here?"

Jennifer's rage was instinctive. Acting purely on an impulse she immediately regretted, one hand came up and slapped his face. Even before the sound died away, she was aghast. But before she could say a word, Kalim grabbed her hands and held both of them behind her back, arching her body against his while she tilted her head away from the black fury on his face.

"You damn little spitfire, you will pay for that! I will teach you about respect before I have finished with you."

She twisted out of his grasp and backed away, panting, but he advanced mercilessly, his eyes glittering with fury.

"Kalim, I . . . I'm sorry I slapped you. I shouldn't have done that, but . . . but this whole thing is one giant misunderstanding."

His hand shot out and fastened around her wrist like a steel bracelet. "You are wrong. I understand perfectly. You want more money and you think you can get it from me if you play hard to get, is that not so?" His mouth curved contemptuously. "Did they not pay you enough?"

Panic was suspended as she stared at him in confusion. "What are you talking about?" His smile became even more derisive as he eyed her tender curves insolently, not bothering to answer. Slowly his suspicions dawned on her and she turned a bright scarlet. "Surely you don't think I'm a . . ." Her voice trailed off in horror.

His hands spanned her narrow waist, urging her toward him once more. Cynicism had replaced anger and his voice was silky as he said, "We do not need to put it into words. Let us just say that we both know how to give pleasure. It does not matter that you are paid to do so."

His insulting words made Jennifer see red! The urge to slap his arrogant face once more was very strong, but this time she managed to control the impulse. Breathing hard, she pushed his hands away and struggled for composure. "I'm sorry to disappoint you, but I am not here for that purpose and I will thank you to keep your hands off me."

Kalim's eyes narrowed to icy chips. "I do not understand this. You will explain."

"That's what I'm *trying* to do!" A touch of bitterness colored her voice. "I don't know what gave you the impression that I was that kind of a girl."

His frown turned into a scowl. "Do not play the innocent with me! You told me yourself that you were being paid to entertain me, is that not so? You came to me, I did not seek you out."

Jennifer sighed and some of her anger evaporated. "Oh, dear—now I know how wars start. People don't understand each other even when they're speaking the same language." She took a deep breath. "Let me try to clear this up. I work for the city, as I told you, but I'm only a secretary. I usually just do typing and shorthand. When they found out late this afternoon that you were arriving, they picked me to go to the airport because there was no other choice. Everyone else was busy. That's all there was to it. Yes, I'm being paid, but only to be your guide—nothing more."

Kalim's brows were still drawn together but more in perplexity now. "You have some strange customs here. In my country, if a beautiful young girl is sent to a man, he knows exactly what is expected of him. It would be insulting not to . . . bestow special attention upon her." His firm mouth curved finally in a smile.

"Well, you're not in your country," Jennifer said hotly, feeling even the tips of her ears grow pink as she remembered his practiced assault on her senses—and her shameful response.

"That is true, but surely you can see that it was a natural mistake." He shrugged. "So be it." Turning to the ice-filled silver urn, he said, "Shall we have our wine now?"

"What?" she gasped. After the frightful scene they had just been through, how could he even consider calmly sharing a drink?

"It should be quite cold." His amused glance took in her shaken face. "I believe it would do you good."

34

Jennifer hastily smoothed her tousled hair. "No thank you. I have to be leaving."

One peaked eyebrow raised. "We have not had supper yet."

"I'm not hungry and it's getting very late. I . . . I have to go to work in the morning." Her voice trembled in spite of all efforts to prevent it.

Cupping her chin in his hand, he looked penetratingly at her, his black eyes fathomless. "You are frightened of me, aren't you?"

"No, I . . . I really am very tired." Suddenly she realized it was true. The whole evening had been a strain and the traumatic ending to it had left her drained of emotion and shaking with fatigue.

He touched the smudged shadows under her eyes and said gently, "Yes, I have treated you badly, little one. Perhaps I should have known. You are so young, so . . . fragile." His low, caressing voice made her heart beat faster and her long lashes fell before the light in his eyes.

"Please . . . may I go now?" she murmured huskily.

His hand rested lightly on her shining hair for just a moment and then he said, "Yes, I will take you."

"Oh, no, please!" Jennifer cried, in a blind panic to get away from this wildly disturbing man. "I'll get a cab."

Snatching up her coat, she tugged desperately at the doorknob, terrified that he would try to stop her. Her anxiety increased when she saw Habeeb approaching with a questioning look on his dark face, but Kalim halted the man with an impatient shake of his head. As she practically ran out the door, Jennifer's last glimpse wasn't encouraging. The two men were watching her escape with narrowed eyes and Kalim had a thoughtful frown on his face.

In the taxi going home her thoughts were a wild jumble. It wasn't until she was safe in her own apartment that Jennifer tried to make some sense out of them. Why was she so upset? It wasn't the first time that a man had made a pass at her, although, admittedly, this had been the most determined one. But nothing had happened. It was all just a big misunderstanding, so why couldn't she simply laugh it off?

Maybe it was the knowledge of her own body's betrayal. Safely home, she remembered the feeling that had swept over her as Kalim's lips and hands had brought hitherto unknown emotions cascading over her; a shudder ran through Jennifer's slim body, and she gave a small moan and buried her face in the pillow. It was a good thing she would never see him again. She was no match for such a practiced lover. He was a Don Juan with the morals of a billy goat! He would have made love to her tonight and forgotten all about her in the morning. But the image of what that night of love would have been like made her body tingle.

Impatient with herself, Jennifer squeezed her eyes shut to dispel the disturbing picture and punched the pillow under her fevered cheek. But it was a long while before sheer exhaustion took over and her tense limbs relaxed in sleep.

Chapter Two

The office was a beehive of activity when Jennifer got to work the next morning. Every telephone was ringing off the hook and the small staff was working at top speed. Tom Graystock paced the floor, bellowing orders and chain-smoking. When he spied Jennifer, he immediately motioned her into his office.

"Well, how did it go last night?" he demanded.

"Fine." Her answer was cautiously noncommittal.

"Fine? What do you mean fine?" he exploded. "Tell me what happened."

"I met him at the airport," she said evenly. "I took him on a little tour of the city and then I delivered him back to his hotel."

"Lord, give me strength!" His eyes turned heavenward. "I *know* that much—give me the details! Did he like San Francisco? Did he say anything we can quote? Does he plan to come back?"

"I think he enjoyed himself," she replied carefully, "but I don't remember him saying anything memorable, and he didn't mention any future plans."

He looked at her in disgust. "The chauffeur could have told me more than that."

She moistened her lips. "I'm sorry, but there really

isn't anything to tell." Kalim's dark eyes seemed to be watching her with derisive amusement and Jennifer shifted restlessly. In a way, she was doing her boss a favor by not giving him the details of that fateful evening. He would probably have a stroke if he knew how it had ended!

"At least tell me where you took him so they don't duplicate it today," Graystock sighed.

That, at least, was firm ground and Jennifer described their sight-seeing tour. Prodded by his questions, she was able to supply enough information to lighten Graystock's gloom and finally escape to her own desk in the outer office.

It was a busy day and Jennifer was grateful for the heavy work load, even though it didn't completely obliterate Kalim from her mind. His memory would return at the strangest times, causing her to stop in the middle of whatever she was doing and stare out the window without really seeing the crowded streets below. Graystock caught her at it once and his gaze was both shrewd and appraising, but mercifully he made no comment.

It was late afternoon when he called her into his office and told her to sit down. Leaning back in his chair, he twirled a pencil around in his fingers and looked at her impassively. "All right, now suppose you tell me what really happened last night."

Startled, she could only stare at him. "I don't know what you mean."

"Yes you do. Is there any reason why you don't want to talk about it?"

Jennifer's fingers were icy as she clasped them tightly in her lap. He obviously knew something, but what? Had Kalim denounced her in some way? But what could he have said? He could hardly have complained that she wouldn't go to bed with him. The memory of his determined efforts in that direction though brought bright color to her cheeks and she ducked her head.

When it became clear that she was struggling for words, Graystock cleared his throat. "Jennifer, I feel responsible for this because I'm the one who threw you two together." He leaned across the desk, and although his embarrassment was evident, he plowed doggedly on. "He didn't . . . I mean, you two . . ."

Her answer was explosive. "No! I told you nothing happened and I meant it. How could you even think such a thing?"

He relaxed and there was relief on his face. "I'm sorry, but I'm fond of you, Jenny—you know that by now. I don't often play the heavy, but when his request came in, it seemed so strange."

She looked at him uncomprehendingly. "What request?"

"Kalim Al Kahira wants to take you to Cairo with him tomorrow morning."

"What?" Jennifer shot out of her chair, her mouth shaped in an oval of disbelief.

"Wait, hear me out. It seems his secretary had an attack of appendicitis and was rushed to the hospital last night. With the big conference coming up and all the delegates starting to gather, it leaves him short-handed. You evidently told him you're a secretary and he said he was impressed by your qualifications."

Jennifer could just imagine the sardonic twist to his mouth when he said that! "That's very flattering, but I'm sure he can hire any number of secretaries in Cairo."

"You'd think so, wouldn't you? But something you said put a bug in his ear and he considers your services indispensable."

Jennifer was mystified. "What did I say?"

"Something about people not understanding each

other even when they spoke the same language." Her breathing quickened as she remembered the circumstances under which those words were uttered, but she didn't have time to dwell on it as he continued. "This conference is Kahira's baby—he's really serious about it. I guess I shouldn't have said what I did about him yesterday. Did he talk about it at all last night?"

"No . . . er, it didn't come up."

"That's surprising." Graystock looked at her appraisingly. "Well, no, maybe it isn't. But anyway, he's determined to set up a world network to take care of these little kids and that takes plenty of money."

"I know it's a worthy project—you don't have to convince me of that. But I just don't see what I have to do with it."

"I was coming to that. Whenever you try to part people from hard cash it's a problem. And the same thing goes for nations. After all, a country is just a group of individuals who have to approve, because when you come right down to it, it's their money. The media is going to cover this conference like a blanket and Kahira doesn't want any misunderstandings. So that's where you come in."

She looked at him blankly. "Where?"

"If there is the slightest loophole—an ambiguous phrase used, for instance—it could give the cheapskates a chance to weasel out of what is really *everyone's* responsibility."

"You won't get an argument from me on that, but I still don't . . ."

"It's very simple," he interrupted, anticipating her question. "Besides wanting you to help out with the secretarial work, Kahira wants to go over the English-language press releases with you. He will tell you what the information *should* say and ask you if the translation conveys the true meaning."

Jennifer collapsed limply in her chair. It was almost

impossible to believe what she was hearing. "I couldn't do a thing like that!"

"Why not?"

"Well, because . . . I . . . it's much too important." The words tumbled over each other. "I couldn't take the responsibility!"

"You understand plain English, don't you?" he asked impatiently. "All Kahira wants is to discuss it with you—that doesn't sound too difficult to me."

A clear picture rose in Jennifer's mind of Kalim and herself sitting close together in some hotel suite, his enigmatic dark eyes watching her try to concentrate on unfamiliar jargon. Could she bear to be that close to him again, remembering the feel of his powerful body awakening slumbering passions she didn't even know she possessed? And if he tried to make love to her again, could she resist that sensuous mouth that seduced her will or those practiced hands that knew exactly where to caress?

Misunderstanding her silence, Graystock took a milder tone. "There's nothing to be so nervous about, Jenny. Your part in all of this is really minor. But it's a good cause, and if you can help even a little bit to solve a problem that's plaguing the world, it will be worth the effort."

The idea seemed overwhelming. "I don't know if I can," she said slowly.

"If it's any comfort to you, everyone else is struggling with the same problem. But look at it this way—what do you have to lose? A free trip to Egypt doesn't sound bad to me."

Egypt! The reality of it struggled with her disbelief. Jennifer had scarcely been out of California and now she was being offered a fantastic trip to an exotic land, all expenses paid. Was she dreaming? Then the practical side of her nature surfaced.

"Did you say tomorrow? I couldn't possibly be ready

41

that soon. I don't have a passport—and what about clothes?"

Her boss started to chuckle. "Isn't that just like a woman? Offered the chance of a lifetime and the first thing she thinks of is, I don't have a thing to wear."

"Well, it's true," she protested.

"Don't worry about it, Jenny. You can buy whatever you need over there and we'll foot the bill. Within reason, of course," he added prudently. "And as for your passport, that's all being taken care of. The State Department is processing it right now."

Everything was moving too fast and Jennifer had the feeling that she was being steamrollered. It was a fabulous opportunity, of course, and yet . . . why had Kalim requested her services? Was the reason he gave the real one or was there something a great deal more sinister behind all this?

They had scarcely parted friends. The misunderstanding between them had left them both angry. A tiny chill ran up her back even now when she remembered his unleashed fury as he stalked her like a giant cat, bending her trembling body like a reed when he caught her. And what had he said after she slapped his face?—"You will pay for that!"

"What's eating you now?" Graystock complained.

"I was just thinking that this whole thing is too good to be true," she said diffidently. "He could use any American who was already over there. Why me?"

"Oh, for Pete's sake," he exploded, "you're being offered a gift. Why look for strings attached?"

Because Kalim in the role of benefactor didn't ring true, Jennifer thought grimly. No, the more she thought about it, the stranger it seemed. Kalim was a man who wasn't used to being turned down and her rejection couldn't have sat well with his proud nature. His narrowed eyes as she ran out the door were inscrutable, but it didn't take a mind reader to sense his displeasure. Had he decided to forgive and forget? Or did he have some diabolical revenge planned once he got her away from the safety of her own country?

Graystock's impatient voice reminded her of the shortage of time. "If you don't get out of here, you'll never be ready. The plane leaves first thing in the morning."

"I haven't agreed to go yet," she protested.

"Of course you have—it's all settled. Kahira is even sending his man for you. That big bruiser—what's his name?"

Something clicked in Jennifer's mind and she felt as though she had been given a sign. Habeeb! That big bruiser. Kalim had told her himself that Habeeb would carry out any order. He was like a giant robot and she was terrified of him. Her instincts were right when they warned her that something was wrong. The fact that he was part of the package deal was the deciding factor and she wanted none of it.

"No, I've made up my mind." She shook her head. "I'm not going."

"Are you crazy?" He looked at her as though she had taken leave of her senses. "You don't know what you're saying!"

"Yes, I do. I'm telling you that I don't want the job."

"But why, in the name of all that's sensible?" His face showed complete bewilderment.

Jennifer lowered her head and looked carefully at her tightly clasped hands. "The reason doesn't matter, does it?"

"You're really serious, aren't you?" he asked slowly. When she nodded her head, there was a short silence. Looking up, she saw that he was observing her gravely. "I think you ought to reconsider, Jennifer. I don't believe you've thought this whole thing out."

"What do you mean? It's my decision, isn't it?"

"Yes," he admitted, "but have you considered the consequences?"

Now it was her turn to be puzzled. "I don't think I know what you're driving at."

In a mystifying aside Graystock said, "Are you still hoping for a job with that congressman if he gets elected in November?"

Her soft brow furrowed at this sudden change of subject. "You know I am. We talked it all over and you even advised me to take it. You're not having second thoughts, are you?" she asked anxiously. "It will be a snap to train somebody to take my place here and you agreed that it was an opportunity I couldn't afford to pass up."

"I still think so and that's the point. If you refuse this request from Kahira, you can kiss your career in politics good-bye."

"What does one thing have to do with the other?" she cried.

"Grow up, Jenny. If you don't know that politics is a very involved game, then you're not ready for it. Your services have been requested by a very powerful man. Our government wants to lead the world by giving him our full cooperation, and if there's any chance you can be helpful in Cairo, the State Department is all for it. If you turn him down for no discernible reason, they're going to conclude that you're capricious at best and undependable at worst. There are hundreds of girls who would like to be on a congressman's staff. How much chance do you think you'd have of getting the job if a few disparaging words were used against you?"

"But that's practically blackmail!" she protested.

He shrugged. "Who ever told you life was fair? Now, I'm asking as your friend—is there any good reason why you don't want to go to Egypt?"

Jennifer moistened her dry lips as he waited,

watching her shrewdly. What could she tell him? There wasn't really a valid reason—only her own wild surmises. She couldn't say, I'm afraid of Kalim. He makes my blood race, and when he kissed me, it was like nothing I'd ever experienced before. He's a suave and experienced lover and I don't trust him. I think he means to teach me some kind of lesson.

No, she couldn't tell Mr. Graystock that, but what reason *could* she give? He was right about her job with Congressman Peregrini. With a sinking heart Jennifer realized that no matter how useful she had been to him in the past, he wouldn't want to saddle himself with someone who might turn out to be a liability. Nor would anyone else.

A feeling of hopelessness enveloped her as she felt the trap closing, but there was nothing to do but surrender. "There's no good reason and you're right—I guess I don't have any choice."

"That's a smart girl," Graystock told her approvingly. "As long as Kahira wants you, you're stuck. But look at the bright side. Do you know how many people would jump at the chance to change places with you?"

His first words electrified her and Jennifer barely heard the question that followed. Unwittingly, he had given her the solution to this whole mess. *As long as he wants you*—that was the key! If Kalim withdrew his request, she was off the hook.

Did he know that a suggestion from him would be honored like a command? Surely not. It was another case of people not understanding each other. Although she had a deep-seated feeling that this trip was wrong for her for a variety of reasons, she mustn't make Kalim into a monster.

Last night had been a trying experience and her overwrought nerves were reading all kinds of sinister motives into something that was quite simple. She had inadvertently given him a good idea and he had acted on it. But if she explained that it complicated her life, he would be glad to find someone else. Wouldn't he?

"Are you all right, Jenny?"

Vaguely aware that Mr. Graystock was looking at her anxiously, she managed a little smile. "Of course. May I leave now? I have a million things to do." Not wanting to be talked out of her plan, she was careful not to mention it.

"Sure, go ahead and get packed. I'll phone you later with all the details."

Returning hurriedly to the outer office, Jennifer got her purse from the desk drawer. There were no taxis in sight when she reached the street, but an approaching cable car provided a handy substitute. It was only a short trip up the California Street hill and this would be faster anyway.

The little trolley with its gay red and gold paint looked more like a ride at an amusement park than a public conveyance as it made its imperious way up the street with bells clanging. The jam-packed little car was always filled to the rafters, mostly with tourists clinging to every pole and even standing outside on the steps. Today was no exception.

Jennifer managed to squeeze on board, but she was oblivious to the happy people laughing and chattering all around her. The thoughts running through her mind were somber. Back at the office, her plan to get Kalim to release her had seemed so simple, but her doubts were starting to multiply with each passing block.

Suppose he refused? What if there really *was* an ulterior motive behind all this? There went her wild imagination again, making a big deal out of nothing. Once she explained everything and apologized for any misunderstanding between them, surely everything would be all right.

Suddenly, it struck her. That might be what he wanted all along—an apology! Well, he was certainly entitled to it. The enormity of her actions last night swept over Jennifer. How *could* she have slapped his face? That just wasn't done no matter what the provocation! It didn't help to realize that she was probably the first person to take such a liberty.

When the cable car jerked to a stop on top of Nob Hill, Jennifer got off reluctantly and crossed the cobbled courtyard of the imposing hotel. Using the house phone in the lobby, she listened to the ring with a thumping heart. An unfamiliar voice answered, and after giving her name and receiving permission to go up, she entered the elevator. Unfortunately for her already shaken confidence, Habeeb answered the door.

"I'm here to . . . is . . . may I see Kalim?" she stammered.

The huge man barred her way, not a trace of expression on his threatening countenance. But from an inner room a deep masculine voice called, "Is that the little Jennifer, Habeeb? Bring her in here."

She breathed a sigh of relief and followed the big man, but at the sight of Kalim, her heart did a flip and she hesitated in the doorway. He was shrugging into a white shirt and she stared fascinated at the muscles rippling in his shoulders and the curly black hair on his powerful chest.

When he noticed her hesitation, a mocking light lit his dark eyes. "I am sorry to embarrass you by inviting you into my bedroom, my cautious little virgin. But alas, I must dress to go out."

She caught her breath indignantly. "I won't keep you. I just want a minute of your time."

"I would be willing to give you much more than that," he said, and although the words were courteous, they were said derisively.

Attempting to quell her mounting anger, Jennifer came right to the point. "I came to thank you for your job offer and to tell you that I can't accept."

He didn't look surprised, but his eyes hardened to onyx as he regarded her dispassionately. "May I ask the reason?"

"What difference does it make? I just can't, that's all, and I'd like you to tell the State Department that you've changed your mind."

"But I have not."

His refusal wasn't entirely unexpected, but it was irritating nonetheless. "You don't understand what you're doing," Jennifer told him impatiently.

A sardonic smile touched the corners of his mouth. "I do not?"

She looked at him warily and became a lot less sanguine about the success of her mission. "Look, Kalim, I'm glad you thought I gave you a good idea—about double-checking the news releases, I mean. But you don't need me. I'd like you to choose someone else."

He had resumed dressing and Jennifer was relieved when the crisp white shirt was at last buttoned over his bronze chest. "Why would I do that? I have already chosen you."

His faintly disinterested tone infuriated her, but she carefully kept her voice level. "It isn't convenient for me to go to Egypt right now. I have other plans."

"You will change them." It was a flat statement.

"I will *not!*" she snapped. But when his narrowed eyes bored into hers, she added hastily, "I mean, I can't."

"I believe you can," he told her, and his smug assurance made her careless.

"Then let's just say I don't want to," she flung at him.

"Perhaps you will tell me why?" His voice was silky, but Jennifer could tell that he wasn't giving way, and she felt a chill, sensing the implacable will of this man.

Ignoring the question, she took a different tack. "I'll

find someone else for you, someone who will be much more suitable." It was an idea that had suddenly popped into her mind, but it would be a snap to accomplish even at such short notice. He refused to take the bait however, merely shaking his head. "Why not?" she cried.

"Let us say that I have made up my mind and I dislike changing it." He smiled.

"But that isn't fair! Why does it have to be me?"

His lazy glance took in every curve of her slim body before moving unhurriedly to the lovely face. "Because I wish it," he answered mockingly.

She felt the blood start to course through her veins at his sensuous appraisal and was furious at his ability to inflame her senses even while she was hating him. "You're being completely unreasonable," she raged. "This is just a whim on your part."

His face hardened. "I am used to indulging my whims."

"Not with me, you're not! I won't go and you can't make me!"

"As you will." He shrugged. "I believe your people have a saying—It is a free country."

Jennifer bit her lip, chagrined at where her temper had led her. Swallowing her pride, she pleaded with him. "Kalim, I haven't told you the whole story. I *can't* turn down your offer—you're the one who has to release me. It's too complicated to explain, but if I don't go with you, the whole career I have planned will be over."

"Perhaps when you see my part of the world you will choose a new career," he said, unmoved.

"As what—a belly dancer to entertain your visiting firemen?" she said, her anger flaring.

His eyes roved insolently over her slender figure. "I think not. You would be considered immature in my country." Jennifer gasped, but before she could explode into recriminations, he continued. "Besides, you are completely untrained. I would have to spend all my time teaching you how to please a man."

Jennifer turned a bright rosy pink and her long lashes drooped before the smoldering light in his eyes. The thought crossed her mind that he didn't need anyone to help interpret the nuances of English—he understood double meanings all too well!

Kalim was regarding her flushed face with amusement. "You have a lovely body, but not for belly dancing. However, if you insist, I will do my best to instruct you."

"Will you forget this nonsense and get back to the subject?" she pleaded.

"I believe you were the one who was inquiring about a new vocation," he told her sardonically.

Jennifer took a deep breath, willing her heartbeat to return to normal. "Kalim, let's be serious. I appreciate your magnificent offer, but I can't accept it."

"That is your right." He inclined his head courteously.

"But it isn't! If you don't tell them you've changed your mind, there is no way I can refuse." When he simply looked at her with a faint smile playing around his mobile mouth, Jennifer realized how wrong she'd been. Kalim was an accomplished strategist. It was unlikely that he would be ignorant of how much power he wielded. "You know that, don't you?" she whispered.

Without bothering to acknowledge the fact, he smoothed her long, wind-tossed hair gently. "You will enjoy Egypt and I will enjoy showing it to you."

Tears misted her eyes. "Please don't do this to me, Kalim," she begged.

"Why are you so afraid of me, little dove?" He cupped her quivering chin in his hand and forced her to look at him. "I will not harm you."

His voice was so soft and reassuring that Jennifer wanted to throw herself into his arms and have them comfort her, which was funny, considering that he was the cause of her misery. With a conscious effort she squared her shoulders instead.

She was a fool to have come here. Kalim would always get his own way. But she mustn't let him know how helpless he made her feel or how powerfully his slightest touch affected her. He would be quick to take advantage of any weakness, especially one shown by a woman. Fortunately, it was only a physical attraction he exerted over her, and that could be battled. Jennifer felt sorry for any girl foolish enough to actually fall in love with him!

She would have to be on her guard every minute with this dangerously attractive man. It was a perilous journey she was about to embark on, but since there was no way out, she would just have to make the best of it.

Drawing a shaky breath, she said, "Okay, you win. What time shall I be ready in the morning?"

Chapter Three

The long flight was more than half over and Jennifer still found it difficult to convince herself that she wasn't dreaming. Looking around the private plane didn't help; it was very different from the commercial planes she had flown in.

Instead of the neatly arranged rows of seats encountered on a normal jet, this plane was broken up into sections. In the front soft armchairs faced each other over wide polished tables. The middle of the plane had long couches lining each wall and only in the back were there conventional tiers of two seats on either side of a narrow aisle.

Kalim sat in front with a sheaf of papers spread on one of the tables. From her place in the very back of the plane Jennifer watched him covertly. No one had told her where to sit, but as the only woman aboard other than the stewardess, she had self-consciously tucked herself away as unobtrusively as possible. Not that any of the men in Kalim's coterie paid any attention to her. I might as well be the invisible woman, she thought rebelliously.

Sighing deeply, Jennifer returned to her book, although by now she was tired of reading. The stewardess brushed by on her way to the galley and on an impulse Jennifer got up to join her. She had met Talia on boarding and the other girl was about her age, tall and dark with a pretty face and a friendly manner. Perhaps she could spare time for a little chat.

Following her to the small compact kitchen, she found the stewardess busily assembling cups and saucers. "Let me help you with that," Jennifer offered.

Looking up in surprise, Talia said, "Oh, no, Miss Fairchild, you're a guest."

"I'd really like to, if you don't mind. I'm so tired of sitting I think my whole body is getting numb."

Talia nodded sympathetically. "It is a long trip, especially when you're not used to it."

"That's why I'd really appreciate having something to do," Jennifer said.

"All right then, you can help me serve the coffee. It isn't very exciting, but it's the best I have to offer."

"I'm so desperate that it sounds positively stimulating." Jennifer laughed.

Talia filled four cups with the strong steaming brew and put them on a tray. Handing it to Jennifer, she said, "You can serve Mr. Kahira and his aides at the table. They like it very hot. I'll take care of the others."

Jennifer would have preferred it the other way around, but after asking for the job, she couldn't very well complain. Lifting the tray, she carried it carefully down the aisle, watching to be sure that none of the coffee slopped over into the saucers.

The four men were immersed in their work and didn't even look up when she placed a cup at each elbow. Congratulating herself on the fact that Kalim hadn't noticed who was doing the serving, she was about to return to the galley when the plane gave a sudden lurch.

In an effort to steady herself Jennifer instinctively grabbed for the nearest solid object, which turned out to be Kalim's shoulder. Her body swayed against his as the plane righted itself and his arm automatically went out to circle her waist.

Glancing up, he registered surprise and then amusement as he noted the flush on her face caused by the small intimacy. "You wished my attention?" he asked.

"No, of course not," she muttered. "The plane dipped and I lost my balance." She struggled to free herself from his embrace. "Will you please let go of me?"

"I do not know if I should. You seem to be somewhat . . . off balance still." From the wicked gleam in his eye Jennifer felt sure he was aware of the double entendre of his words.

"I'm fine now," she assured him haughtily, turning to leave.

He caught her wrist. "Wait. Why are you serving the coffee?"

"I got so tired of sitting that I asked Talia if I could help," she explained so that the stewardess wouldn't get into trouble.

Kalim stood up and stretched with feline grace. In the close confines of the plane Jennifer was uncomfortably aware of the nearness of his lithe body.

"It is a wearisome journey, but it will soon be forgotten once we reach our destination."

"Not by me. I have the return trip to look forward to in just a short time," she pointed out.

His eyes took on a shuttered look as he grasped her elbow, guiding her down the aisle. "Come, let us stretch our legs."

But they had no sooner reached the back of the plane when the stewardess approached saying, "I'm sorry, but we're expecting some turbulence, would you please take a seat?"

They sat down and buckled their seat belts and Kalim said, "It is as well. This will give us a chance to talk."

"About what?"

"About you to begin with."

"I'm sure you could find something more interesting than that," she told him.

"I think not." He gave her an intent look. "Tell me about these plans of yours that I have interrupted."

All of her resentment rushed back and she lowered her head to prevent him from seeing her indignation. "It's not important," she muttered.

"But it is. I wish to know." Under his expert probing she reluctantly revealed the whole story as he observed her closely. "This congressman—he is unattached?"

Jennifer was puzzled by the question. "No, he's married and has two small children."

He leaned back in satisfaction and then remarked, "That is why your boyfriend does not object."

"Boyfriend?" Surprise colored her voice.

"You have no man in your life?"

"I thought you . . . I mean, you sounded like you think I do." Jennifer was confused.

"I did not, but it is obvious that a girl as beautiful as you would have a male admirer—perhaps many of them." His narrowed eyes focused on her thoughtfully.

It was true that a lot of men were attracted to Jennifer, but the problem was, she wasn't attracted to them. Every date seemed to end in the same wrestling match and she was tired of it. It wasn't true that she was cold, as many of her escorts had implied. Remembering Kalim's arms encircling her and his warm hand caressing forbidden areas, she felt a thrill in the pit of her stomach. Fortunately, she had never met anyone quite like him. Would things have been different? Jennifer shivered, unwilling to think about it.

"You are thinking of your boyfriend perhaps?" Kalim's dry voice cut through her reverie.

"Yes," Jennifer lied.

"And yet you do not seem completely happy. Perhaps he does not . . . satisfy you."

"It's nothing like that," she told him angrily.

"Knowing you, I did not think it was," he answered, raising one eyebrow sardonically.

Fury engulfed Jennifer. "Oh, you . . . you . . . " she spluttered. "You wouldn't understand. You judge everyone by yourself."

If Jennifer had hoped to provoke him, she was disappointed. He regarded her with indulgent amusement. "Do you feel you know me well enough to say such a thing?"

"Yes! You're completely unprincipled!" she said, defying him. "You take whatever you want regardless of the cost to anyone else."

His half-closed eyes appraised her lazily. "You are referring to yourself, of course."

"What if I am?" she flared.

"You are being emotional and a wise man does not attempt to reason with an irrational woman."

"You don't bother with reason anyway. Your method is to use force," she told him bitterly.

"That is true." He nodded in calm assent. "But sometimes it is justified. You are too cautious, little dove. I have opened the door of your cage and one day you will thank me. I know what is best for you."

"How could you possibly? We come from different worlds."

"Do you mean that East and West can never meet?"

"Something like that," she challenged.

Tilting her face toward him, he looked at her intently. "Men and women have the same needs the world over."

Something stirred inside of her but she ignored it, saying tartly, "But the men in your part of the world seem to need more women to fulfill those needs."

He threw back his head and laughed aloud, his white teeth gleaming in the bronzed handsome face. "I doubt if any man could have as many amorous adventures as you are crediting to me, little one."

"I suppose you'd have me believe you're celibate."

"Heaven forbid!"

"When a man says that, it's considered dashing," she commented bitterly, "but how many women could say the same thing?"

"If your inexperience bothers you, I would be glad to volunteer my services."

"Oh . . . you . . . you're impossible!" she gasped.

His laughter bubbled over and he lifted her hand to his lips. "I hope you are as delightful in bed as you are to tease."

She snatched her hand away furiously. "*You* will never find out!"

"Do not challenge me, Jennifer." His voice was gentle but it hid veiled menace. "You might find you are—how do you say it—outmatched."

The ominous words struck a chill to Jennifer's heart. She had spent a sleepless night puzzling over his intentions and suddenly felt unable to fence with him any longer.

"I don't think this conversation is getting us anywhere and I'm very tired," she told him stiffly.

Looking at her closely, he noticed the circles under her eyes. "Yes, you must get some rest, little one. A whole new world awaits you."

Uncoiling his great length, Kalim reached into the compartment overhead and brought out a pillow and a blanket. Tipping her seat back so that it was almost horizontal, he tucked the cushion under her head and began to cover her.

"You don't have to do that. I can take care of myself, thank you," Jennifer protested primly, but when she started to sit up he held her down easily.

Looking hypnotically into her eyes, he said in a low voice, "Do not try to struggle against your fate, little dove—you cannot win." And lifting her hand, he pressed a kiss into the palm.

She watched him walk swiftly down the aisle and her fingers closed involuntarily. Cradling her hand protectively under her cheek, she soon fell asleep.

An intangible change of tempo awoke Jennifer and she opened her eyes to increased activity aboard the plane.

"I was just going to wake you, Miss Fairchild," Talia told her. "We're about to land."

Jennifer put her seat back up and stared out the window, excitement chasing the sleep from her foggy brain. A fairyland had appeared out of nowhere and was spread out beneath the small pane of glass. Tall modern buildings jostled against domed minarets and the setting sun gilded palacelike structures straight out of the *Arabian Nights*. As the plane swooped lower, she saw pink mimosa trees blossoming in the very heart of the city. All at once it struck her—she was in Egypt, land of the Pharaohs!

Even after the plane touched down on the runway Jennifer remained glued to the window, excitement oozing out of every pore. She didn't know how long Kalim had been standing over her, but when she looked up his deep voice prompted, "It is time to go." And taking his extended hand in a kind of daze, she followed him out into the Egyptian twilight.

The warm blast of air that hit her seemed somehow fitting. San Francisco with its fog and cool climate was half a world away. This was the mysterious Middle East and she felt like pinching herself to prove she was really here.

Resting his arm lightly around her shoulders, Kalim smiled down at her. "I was not wrong. Already you feel the pulsating beat of my country."

"It's very exhilarating," she had to admit.

The same confusion greeted their arrival that had reigned in San Francisco and Jennifer reflected that some things were the same all over the globe. But once they were settled in the limousine, everything was different. She perched precariously on the edge of the seat and drank in the passing scenery, asking insatiable questions without giving him a chance to reply.

"Kalim, what is the name of that mosque? Oh, look at that adorable child—what do you call that kind of gown he's wearing? What's that big building over there with the golden dome?"

Finally Kalim reached out and drew her back against him. "Patience, my love. I shall answer all your questions as you did mine. The Egyptian Museum contains four thousand items from the tomb of Tutankhamen. They were removed from Thebes fifty years ago and . . ."

She interrupted him, laughing. "Is that what I did to you?"

"I did not mind." He gazed at her teasingly. "I could look at your beautiful face and imagine a conclusion to the evening that never took place."

His voice was gently mocking and Jennifer was suddenly aware of his arms cradling her against his hard body. Blushing furiously, she pulled away. "You've been all over the world, so one more place is no big deal," she told him, ignoring his suggestive comment. "But I've never been anywhere and I really do want to know all about Egypt."

"And so you shall," he said. "I promise."

Their car drew up before a stately hotel and all conversation was necessarily at an end for the time being. Jennifer had already witnessed the service accorded to this man, but she was overwhelmed once more, especially since she was sharing in it this time. Bellmen whisked their luggage away and bowing doormen ushered them into a lobby that was stunning in its opulence. Taking in the mosaic floors and gilded statues, Jennifer practically wriggled with delight. Say what you will, it was nice to be part of a millionaire's entourage!

While she was looking around and enjoying her moment of reflected glory, a female body came hurtling across the lobby and threw itself into Kalim's arms.

"Darling, I thought you would never get here!"

The newcomer was a stunning brunette. Her glossy black hair swept across her smooth tanned shoulders and the black eyes that she turned on Kalim were limpid with adoration. Her sensuous figure molded to his as though it were a habit and her arms twined confidently about his neck.

"Ayesha, my dear!" There was delight in the voice that greeted her. "I did not know you were going to be here."

"If you had called me as you promised, I would have told you," she pouted.

He held her away from him and laughed into her upturned eager face. "No amount of attention would satisfy you, cherie, so I have given up."

"Well, I have not," she said, pulling his head down to hers.

Kalim kissed her lightly before firmly disentangling her clinging arms. "Ayesha, you are a spoiled child. Have you no shame at this public display?" but his voice was softly indulgent.

"None at all," she answered cheerfully, linking arms with him and hugging him close to her body. "Come along—you have kept us waiting much too long."

Jennifer watched helplessly as the other girl started to tug Kalim toward the bank of elevators. With Ayesha's appearance he seemed to have forgotten everything else. What am I supposed to do now? Jennifer wondered, feeling abandoned and curiously bereft. But Kalim wasn't completely bewitched after all.

"You will have to control your impatience, cherie," he told the dark-haired girl. "There are things to be done before I can give you my undivided attention." Turning to Jennifer, he said, "May I have your passport please?"

It was a moment before Ayesha realized that Jennifer was connected in some way with Kalim. But once it registered her eyes narrowed in a thorough appraisal. Jennifer felt pale and wan before this flashing beauty who never released her proprietary grip on an unresisting Kalim. So this was the kind of woman he preferred. Like all men, he would make a pass at anything that might be available, but this volatile, curvaceous Venus was his real choice.

"Your passport?" Kalim's impatient voice recalled her attention.

Jennifer started to open her purse and then stopped. She had always heard that you should never let your passport out of your sight. "Why do you want it?" she asked suspiciously.

"It is necessary to surrender it at the registration desk," he explained. When she continued to look doubtful, he added, "I assure you it is the custom in every country."

Jennifer flushed under his sardonic look, aware that she had revealed her lack of sophistication. But it was no crime to be ignorant of foreign ways, she told herself angrily. Undoubtedly, the glamorous well-traveled Ayesha knew everything there was to know, so why didn't he just go off with her?

Raising her chin haughtily, Jennifer said, "I can take care of it myself. I wouldn't want to detain you."

Kalim's eyes turned cold and his mouth tightened. "Will you stop acting like a little fool?"

Jennifer's spine stiffened, but before she could answer Ayesha tugged on Kalim's arm, asking suspiciously, "Who is she?" as though Jennifer were an inanimate object.

"I am sorry. Where are my manners?" As Kalim made the introductions, he was once more the suave, poised male, regarding the two girls with an amused understanding.

Jennifer acknowledged the introduction politely, but Ayesha turned to Kalim and spoke rapidly in a foreign tongue.

"You will speak in English," Kalim told her evenly. "Jennifer does not understand our language. In answer to your question, she is my . . . aide."

Ayesha's sulky mouth expressed both jealousy and displeasure, but a steely quality about Kalim warned her to keep silent. Even his favorite had to toe the line, Jennifer noted gleefully, but her small triumph faded rapidly. Ayesha undoubtedly had her own special way of getting around him when they were alone.

Kalim took care of their registration in a minimum of time for which Jennifer was devoutly grateful, although she still felt doubtful about relinquishing her passport. The small booklet was her only tie to home and she felt very alien in this exotic country where one person had already made her feel like an intruder.

Ayesha's manners in no way matched her beauty. While Kalim was busy at the desk, she withdrew a small mirror from her purse and examined her flawless complexion, not even making a pretext at polite conversation. When he finished his business, her charm returned.

Going up in the elevator, she bubbled over with bits of gossip and by turning slightly managed to isolate herself and Kalim. Jennifer was aware of being regarded as a nuisance, probably by Kalim as well, and she inched her way uncomfortably toward the back of the car.

"Do you feel unwell, Jennifer?"

She looked up to see his intent gaze scanning her face. "No, I'm fine," she said in a small voice.

The elevator stopped at their floor and he took her arm, oblivious to the quick hiss of rage from the dark-haired girl on his other side.

"I will see you to your room and you can refresh yourself," he told Jennifer.

"Kalim, everyone is waiting in your suite," Ayesha protested. "We are having a welcoming party for you."

They were approaching an open door where loud music and the sound of many voices could be heard— the party had evidently started without him. But Kalim's arrival was announced by a lookout and a horde of beautifully dressed men and women erupted into the corridor, greeting him in several different languages.

Once more Jennifer was the outsider and felt like she was intruding, although no one even noticed her. She sighed. There was nothing to do but wait until Kalim remembered her existence—if he ever did! Why hadn't she asked for the key so she could slip away to her own room? Shrinking into a corner was becoming a habit, Jennifer reflected bitterly. But she wasn't as invisible as she supposed.

Spotting her hovering uncertainly on the fringes, one of the men left the chattering group and approached, eyeing her charms appreciatively. Taking her completely by surprise, he captured both of her hands, gave her a radiant smile, and proceeded to rattle off a fast stream of French. Since her knowledge of that language was minimal, she couldn't decide whether he was telling her she had lovely hair or that the weather was beautiful. While her soft brow furrowed and she was trying to disentangle herself, Kalim plowed through the crowd of well-wishers.

"Do not allow René to alarm you," he laughed, pulling her gently to his side. "He is quite harmless."

"The little golden doll is English!" René exclaimed, in her language this time.

"No, I'm American," she told him.

"Ah, America! I have visited your land and it is *très magnifique*. We must have a long talk about it."

"Later, René," Kalim advised. "The little golden doll"—he looked down at her in amusement as he repeated René's endearment—"has had a long journey. She wishes to unpack her clothing." He looked over the crowded corridor and as though by magic Habeeb appeared. It was a little spooky, Jennifer thought as Kalim said, "Habeeb will take you to your room."

She stiffened against him. "No! I . . . I can find my own way."

For a moment his arm tightened protectively, as though he sensed her unspoken fear. Then he said softly, "Trust me, little one. And trust Habeeb."

There was nothing else for her to do but to follow the giant. Fortunately, her room was only at the end of the hallway, and after unlocking the door, he quietly handed her the key. She thanked him haltingly, but he merely inclined his head before moving off in that silent way that was so amazing considering his size.

The room assigned to her was so luxurious that Habeeb was immediately erased from her mind. A huge king-sized bed dominated one wall, but what made it memorable was the lush canopy over it, a peaked awning suitable for sheltering royalty. Ceiling-high windows were draped in peacock blue satin to match the swagged folds over the bed and the thick carpet was in the same blue surrounding a pattern of deep red roses. There were comfortable chairs and tables scattered about the spacious room and a wide seat heaped with pillows was built into the recess of the tall windows.

A partially opened door revealed a modern bathroom with a sunken marble tub and an oval sink inlaid with Egyptian figures in blue and deep rose.

After Jennifer had inspected every inch of her temporary domain, she ran a bath, adding some of the scented bath salts that were on the ledge. While the huge tub was filling, she unpacked and shed her traveling clothes, feeling as though she had worn them for weeks instead of the long weary hours it had been. Standing in front of the mirror, she pinned her long thick hair on top of her head, careless of the silky little curls that escaped at the nape of her neck.

A long soak in the fragrant water relaxed her completely. Climbing out, she toweled dry. A thin cotton robe provided more than enough covering in the warm Egyptian climate.

As she tied the sash around her slender waist, a knock sounded and she paused uncertainly. Who could that be? Opening the door a fraction, she was surprised to see Kalim.

"I came to see if your accommodations were adequate," he informed her.

"Oh, yes! They're perfectly beautiful," she assured him.

Pushing the door open, he brushed past her. "I wish to see for myself."

Jennifer pulled her robe together nervously, uncomfortably aware of the fact that it was quite thin and she wore nothing under it. "This really isn't necessary."

"I believe it is." He regarded her cynically. "Would you complain if your room were not comfortable?"

"No, I guess not," she admitted. "But all of this is a delightful surprise. I would have been happy with much less."

"You are easily satisfied."

"It comes from not being to the manor born," she told him dryly.

"Meaning?" His eyebrows rose questioningly.

"Meaning that I'm not accustomed to the luxury you take for granted."

Moving closer in order to watch her reaction, he said, "You resent my position, do you not?"

The room was very quiet and Jennifer was quiveringly aware of the fact that they were alone in her bedroom and she was practically unclothed. Would it have been as distracting a situation with anyone else? Or was it Kalim? She only knew that being so close to his tall, muscular body, so blatantly male, was making her bare legs tremble.

Attempting to keep the knowledge from him, she forced her voice to remain casual. "Of course I don't resent it. If I had been asked, I'm sure I would have chosen to be born rich."

He shrugged. "A woman does not have to be born rich. She can always marry money."

"I've heard that's the hardest way to earn it."

A mocking smile tilted the corners of his mouth. "Some women might not agree with you."

Ignoring his impudent tone, she said, "Besides, the average girl doesn't stand much chance of meeting a millionaire."

"I am not really interested in the average girl. Let us talk about you—would you like the idle life of the rich wife?"

That, at least, was easy to answer and she shook her head. "I don't think I could ever just sit around and do nothing no matter how much money I had."

"Don't women spend a lot of time having their hair done?" His derisive tone made her bristle.

"I wouldn't know," she told him. "I do my own."

"Amazing!" He reached out and took a strand of her hair, winding it around his finger like a shining gold band. His light touch was tantalizing and Jennifer moved away from his disturbing hands, but he closed the distance between them, adding, "I have also heard that ladies can occupy themselves for many hours over lunch and shopping."

"Some do," she admitted, "but it sounds deadly to me."

"Then what would you do with yourself if you did not have to make your own living?" he persisted.

Wondering why he was finding her likes and dislikes so interesting, she nevertheless thought it over. "Oh, I'd like to travel, of course, but I'd also want to be involved in something important. Working with the handicapped perhaps or getting involved in this children's project you're putting together. That's really so worthwhile."

His eyes suddenly darkened. "Yes, the little ones of the world do not deserve their fate."

Gazing at his somber face, Jennifer was ashamed of ever having doubted his sincerity. He might be ruthlessly male when it came to women or business, but his dedication to defenseless children was clearly evident. What a strange man he was!

She touched his sleeve tentatively, wanting to lighten his mood. "But you, at least, are doing something about it and I think that's truly wonderful."

A dancing light appeared in his dark eyes, chasing away the shadows. "If that is true, then why was it so difficult to persuade you to come here?" he teased.

As if he didn't know! But Jennifer refused to be drawn into a discussion that would leave her on the defensive. Besides, now was the time to say something that had been on her mind.

"Kalim, you and I might not always get along, but I believe with all my heart in what you're trying to do and I just want you to know that I'm going to do everything I can to help." A curious smile curved his lips and, misinterpreting it, she stiffened and added defensively, "I realize I'm completely ignorant about it now, but I intend to learn. I'm not like your luncheon-going socialite friends."

An unreadable emotion flickered in his dark eyes. "I was aware of that from the first and I was not laughing at you, Jennifer. I was thinking . . . something quite different." And then the teasing smile reappeared. "So you do not fancy being a rich man's plaything?"

"Never! Just keeping a man happy isn't a full-time job."

"Would that not depend on the man?" His tone was definitely suggestive this time.

"Oh! Why do I ever bother to answer you seriously?" she cried. "You have a one-track mind!"

His sensuous glance took in her flushed face and tousled hair. "Perhaps it is your fault for looking so adorably provocative."

"I don't consider that a compliment," Jennifer said scornfully. "You consider all women irresistible!"

"Do I indeed?" he murmured. "Or do you perhaps underrate yourself?"

The throbbing note in his voice lit tiny flames of desire and her response to his blatant masculinity shocked and frightened her. And from the amused look on his face, Jennifer was afraid that he was aware of it.

Her composure was rapidly disappearing and she backtracked in earnest this time, afraid that if he touched her again he would be able to tell how fast her heart was beating. It seemed imperative to put distance between them. But in her haste, disaster fell as the edge of a low table struck her just below the knees, throwing her off balance.

Flinging her arms out, she caught at Kalim, who reached out to steady her. As she swayed toward him, her sash untied and the thin robe flew open.

His arms closed automatically around her and Jennifer, unable to right herself, was thunderously aware of the feel of his hands sliding over her bare body. In the heart-stopping moment that it took to regain her balance, she was aware of his firm muscular thighs thrusting against hers and the feel of his hard chest through the thin silk shirt he wore pressing against her breasts.

An avalanche of emotion swept over her, making her even more frantically embarrassed and she struggled to free herself, but his arms tightened around her. The hands that had reached out to steady her were now aware of their unexpected prize and they stroked her nakedness slowly and sensuously. The feeling was indescribable.

A fire that seemed to start at her toes spread upward through her trembling legs and her awakened body was achingly aware of his maleness. As his warm hands curved over her hips and thighs, Jennifer couldn't restrain a small gasp of pleasure.

"Yes, my darling, give in to it," Kalim murmured huskily, his lips trailing down her throat to the soft hollow between her breasts.

Jennifer wound her arms around his waist, her hands moving across his muscular back as a hunger and a wildness filled her. Those expert caresses were carrying her to a peak of passion she had never visited before and she trembled in anticipation, craving the fulfillment only he could give.

But somewhere reason triumphed, although the voice that announced it didn't seem to belong to her. "Kalim, let me go," she pleaded brokenly.

He looked at her with drugged eyes and his hands molded her hips, pulling them closer to his. "You are so exquisite. I knew you would be like this."

The feelings aroused by slow movement of his body against hers were almost unbearable in their ecstasy. She wanted to throw her arms around his neck and hold him even closer, beg him to make love to her. It was only the training of a lifetime plus superhuman effort that enabled her to struggle against the fatal desire and say instead, "Kalim, you mustn't. This wasn't part of the . . ."

But his mouth silenced her protest. Pulling her gently back to him, his lips claimed hers as though they belonged to him. When she tried to deny his superior strength, one hand fastened around the back of her head, forcing her mouth against his while he parted her lips with a warm probing male dominance.

Jennifer shuddered as a wave of yearning ran over her traitorous body and he gave a low growl of pleasure. His other hand moved up to caress the soft curve of her breast and the tender exploration left her weak.

She clung to him, accepting his kisses and returning them as she never had with any man before. When his palm made slow, sensuous circles on the vulnerable point of her breast, Jennifer cried out in delight, and he crushed her close, murmuring endearments into her neck.

Her fingers tangled in his thick dark hair, glorying in the smell and feel of it, and his hands slid up her sides, drawing her naked body against his. Tearing open his shirt, he moved her breasts slowly back and forth against his bare chest.

The exquisite sensation breached her last defense and she allowed her quivering body to surrender to his hard urgent need for her. Exulting over her crumbling defenses, he lifted her effortlessly in his arms and carried her to the bed, laying her down tenderly. For an earth-shattering moment he knelt above her, and Jennifer stole a look at him through long lashes that veiled a sudden modesty.

There was molten passion on his face, tempered with something that looked almost like regret as his lips kissed the pulse beating wildly in her throat and then slid to the rose-tipped breast that begged his attention. "Forgive me, my darling, I am only human."

As Jennifer reached up to curl an arm around his neck, there was a loud knock at the door. For a moment the intrusion had no meaning. They were on an island in Eden and there was no world outside of themselves and the pleasure they gave each other. Then the knock sounded again, accompanied this time by a shrill voice.

"Kalim! Are you in there?"

It was the voice of Ayesha and it affected them both, but in different ways. Jennifer returned to reality with a shuddering jolt. Grabbing the edge of the spread and dragging it desperately over her nakedness, she looked up in horror. But whether at him or herself, she wasn't quite sure.

How had a thing like this happened? How had she *allowed* it to? Curling into a tight ball, she buried her face in the pillow while wave after wave of shame washed over her. If it hadn't been for that interruption . . . She couldn't bear to think about it!

Dimly she was aware of Kalim's indrawn breath and the fact that he was moving toward the door as the knock came again.

"Ayesha, my dear, were you looking for me?" The deep voice held no hint of embarrassment.

How could he, Jennifer wondered? How could he act as if nothing had happened after making such passionate love to her just a moment ago? Her body still pulsed with shameful desire for him, but he evidently felt nothing. How could he turn off his emotions as one would turn off a water tap?

Was it possible that the longing had all been on her side and he was merely accommodating her as men are always ready to do? The thought turned Jennifer's heart to lead and with a feeling of loathing she tightened the covers over the soft breast that his warm mouth had tasted.

Ayesha's voice was sulky. "I didn't wish to disturb you, but we are going out to dinner now."

"You could never disturb me." Kalim's voice was warm. "As a matter of fact, my childhood friend, you could not have arrived at a better time. Come, let us join the others."

Their voices receded down the hall and Jennifer lowered her listening head, unwilling to believe her ears. She had her answer, but it was too denigrating to think about. He was *happy* that Ayesha had interrupted them before anything irrevocable had happened between them.

Was he afraid Jennifer might have gotten the silly idea that he was in love with her? Not likely! She would just have joined the long list of women who had shared his bed. Women to be enjoyed and forgotten the next morning.

She ought to be grateful to Ayesha, and she was— but so was he! Ayesha had saved him from facing an awkward aftermath. Jennifer was here to do a job, and although his male lust was automatically stimulated by the sight of a nude female body, he didn't really want any entanglements when it came to business.

How would she ever face him again, remembering her abject surrender? He wouldn't realize the enormity of what had almost happened. Kalim would think this was her normal behavior. How could she convince him that she didn't fall into bed with every handsome man she met? Had *never* fallen into bed with one as a matter of fact!

No, it was hopeless—the whole situation was. She was right in feeling she should never have come. The only solution was to go home immediately. Never mind the sticky situation that might arise. It would work out or it wouldn't. At the moment, she couldn't care less. The important thing was to get away.

She would tell Kalim in the morning that she was returning to America and he could like it or lump it! Judging by his relieved greeting to Ayesha, he wouldn't make any trouble.

As soon as she had made a decision, Jennifer's wild panic subsided and a measure of calm returned. Nothing could erase the terrible shame and guilt, but at least she had a plan in mind and the knowledge that her ordeal would soon be over.

Glancing at the clock, she saw that it was getting late. She hadn't had any dinner, but the change in time and her rebellious stomach rejected the idea of food. Much better to get a good night's sleep in order to face tomorrow's long return trip.

Sleep was washing over her and relaxing her tired limbs when a niggling thought teased her back to consciousness—Kalim had never returned her passport. She would have to track it down and retrieve it in the morning.

On that disquieting note Jennifer drifted into oblivion.

Chapter Four

Jennifer opened her eyes reluctantly the next morning, unconsciously bracing herself to face the arduous day ahead. But when she glanced drearily at the clock, an unpleasant surprise caused her to sit bolt upright in bed. Was it really almost noon? How could she possibly have slept so late after all those good intentions about making an early start? It probably had something to do with the time change and the fact that her body hadn't adjusted to it yet. Wasn't there about thirteen hours' difference between Cairo and San Francisco? After futilely trying to make the calculation, she gave up in disgust. What difference did it make? The main thing was to get out of here as quickly as possible!

After a quick shower, she dressed rapidly and sped down to the lobby. For once the front desk wasn't its usual madhouse of activity and a smiling clerk came forward to greet her.

"I'd like my passport back," Jennifer told him, hoping her firm tone would convey a confidence she was far from feeling.

He nodded pleasantly and opened a deep drawer. But when he shuffled through a whole assortment of papers and the magic booklet wasn't forthcoming,

Jennifer's apprehension started to mount. Slowly the man's smile faded, and with a murmured apology he excused himself and disappeared into the back office.

She waited numbly, trying to control her rising panic, but when the clerk returned he was smiling. "All is well, Miss Fairchild. Mr. Kahira has already retrieved your passport."

Oh, no! All is *not* well, she wanted to tell him. In fact, all couldn't be worse! Last night Jennifer had lulled herself to sleep with the thought that she would never have to see Kalim again. It had seemed so simple. By this time she had fully expected to be on a plane for home, and if everything had gone according to plan, she would have been packed and gone before he had the slightest inkling. But when one thing went wrong, everything followed suit.

With a sinking heart Jennifer turned toward the elevator. It wasn't that she anticipated any trouble with Kalim, it was just that she didn't know if she could summon the strength to face him. Not after last night.

Her feet dragged reluctantly down the carpeted corridor and she had to force herself to knock on his door. What if Ayesha were with him? What if they . . . Banishing the churning images that tied her stomach in knots, Jennifer set her chin and rapped firmly on the door.

It was answered almost at once by Habeeb, who took a swift look at her set face and stepped aside for her to enter.

Kalim was seated at a table near the window, a scattering of papers spread out in front of him, and Jennifer noted with relief that he was alone. A damask-covered trolley table with the remains of his breakfast was pushed into a corner and Kalim was dressed in white slacks and a pale blue shirt that accentuated his deep tan.

As she advanced grimly into the room, he sprang up,

eyes alight. "Jennifer, my dear, I did not think you would be up yet—the change in time. I did not wish to disturb you. Did you rest well?"

She looked at him in amazement! Of all the receptions she had steeled herself for, this wasn't one of them. How could he possibly act as though nothing had happened between them? And almost immediately the answer presented itself. Last night had been cataclysmic for her, but for him it had been an unimportant little incident that hadn't quite come off, and rightfully so. His relief was insultingly evident.

Refusing to play games, Jennifer came right to the point. "I've come for my passport."

The eagerness died out of his eyes and the hands that had been reaching for her wavered. "I do not understand."

"It's quite simple. I'm going home—today if I can get a plane."

"But why?"

If Jennifer hadn't known better, she could almost have believed in his bewilderment, he sounded so genuinely perplexed. Which only increased her contempt. Why couldn't he be as honest with her as she was being with him?

"You know perfectly well why and I'd rather not discuss it. My passport please."

"Jennifer, my dearest." He put his hands on her shoulders and her treacherous body remembered their imprint. Trembling, she tried to wrench away, but he held her fast. "I am so sorry about last night."

"I'm sure you are. Did your girl friend give you a bad time or were you able to convince her that it was only a momentary *aberration!*" She spat the last word at him.

Kalim's eyes narrowed and his fingers suddenly tightened. "What are you saying?"

"I realized from the beginning that Ayesha had you on a very short leash, so if you're in real trouble, I'll be glad to give you a note saying absolutely nothing happened," she said scornfully to hide the pain that was twisting her heart.

Kalim's eyes were like chips of ice as he released her. "You think I left you last night because of Ayesha?"

"I don't want to talk about it and I shouldn't think you would either." Jennifer's composure, such as it was, threatened to desert her, but she held herself under tight rein. "Just give me my passport so I can get out of here."

"You really intend to return home?" His dark eyes examined her set face.

"That's exactly right," she snapped.

A marked change came over him. Folding his arms, Kalim lounged against the table and looked at her without expression. "And what will happen to all those plans that you told me would be in jeopardy if you did not accompany me?"

"I don't care anymore!" she cried. "My life will never be the same anyway—isn't that enough for you?" Even as the words tumbled out, she was aware of how melodramatic they sounded, but she was beyond caring.

A small smile touched his lips. "I think you are being a little dramatic. Is it possible that no man has ever seen your beautiful body—or touched it?"

His caressing voice brought flames to her cheeks. "Oh . . . you . . . you're despicable! I hope I never see you again as long as I live."

"That should prove rather difficult." One eyebrow raised derisively. "Since the conference will start in a few days, you will see quite a lot of me."

"Didn't you hear what I said?" she cried in outrage. "I'm going home."

A frown creased his forehead and he looked imperiously at her. "You are not going anywhere. You will stay until I give you permission to leave."

Jennifer felt a searing anger flood through her. "Just whom do you think you're talking to? I'm not one of your peasant girls to be ordered around like a possession. You don't own me!"

"Do not put ideas into my head." His mouth curved cruelly as he looked her up and down. "You would be quite a . . . souvenir to bring home to my estate in Luxor. Little girls with pale hair like yours are much prized in this part of the world. Our women are beautiful, but they are dark and passionate. You, my cold little friend, might be an intriguing change."

A sudden chill ran through Jennifer, but she set her teeth grimly. "If you don't give me my passport this very instant, I'm going to the American Embassy."

"And tell them what?" His tone was cynical. "You can scarcely claim I kidnapped you since your trip was arranged by your own State Department."

"I'll tell them the truth." At his amused stare she faltered. "I mean, I'll tell them you won't let me go, that you're keeping me here against my will."

Kalim lit a long, slender brown cigarette and lifted his chin to watch the smoke spiral toward the ceiling. "And then your American official and I would have to confer on what to do about these delusions of yours. He would not welcome unfortunate publicity on the eve of the conference when the eyes of the world are focused on Cairo. I have no doubt that I could easily convince him it would be best to seek discreet treatment for you here. A private sanitarium perhaps."

"You wouldn't!" Her voice was a horrified whisper.

Kalim shrugged. "You believe everything else about me, why would you doubt that?"

Jennifer felt the room closing in around her. Kalim had won again. She was caught in a trap and every time she tried to get away he tightened it a little bit more just to be sure she got the message. What on earth was she going to do?

As if indicating that the interview was at an end, Kalim turned back to his desk. For a moment she could only stare at his formidable back. Then, with tears blurring her eyes, she turned and ran out of the room and down endless flights of stairs.

Speeding across the mosaic tiled floor of the lobby, Jennifer was unaware of anything except an urgent need to escape. It followed her through the revolving doors, but when the brilliant Cairo sun hit her, she blinked like someone coming out of a trance. Where was she going? Traffic noises assailed her ears and a toothless old man plucked insistently at her sleeve with dirty, clutching fingers. Even as Jennifer shrank away, the doorman dispatched him with fierce, unintelligible words and she escaped down the street and mingled with the crowd, finding solace in anonymity.

At first, misery engulfed her like a noxious cloud and she concentrated on nothing except putting one foot in front of the other. One block merged into another, unnoticed by the desolate girl. But gradually the vitality of the city intruded on her wretchedness, refusing to be ignored.

Cairo was a city of opposites. Men in long enveloping burnooses kept pace with their counterparts in beige linen suits just as modern skyscrapers rubbed elbows with ancient buildings decorated by craftsmen long gone. Automobiles snarled their outrage at the out-moded donkey carts and honked raucously at the occasional camel.

Jennifer was fascinated in spite of herself, and as she wandered through the teeming streets, the wonder of this urgent, seething city gripped her. Without knowing or caring where she was going, she drifted with the crowd, watching the fascinating mixture of people, listening to snatches of conversation, and glancing into shop windows.

Suddenly, her eye was caught by the pink mimosa

trees she had seen from the plane—or else some very like them. They were spreading their glory across the front of the Egyptian Museum and she gravitated naturally toward the entrance.

The traveling Tutankhamen show had been in San Francisco a short time previously and Jennifer, like the rest of the country, had been dazzled by its splendor. She had heard that the artifacts on tour were only a tiny fraction of what was left behind and now was her opportunity to see the rest of the collection.

Entering the stately museum was like walking back into history. The lighting was poor and the floor was cracked in places, but it seemed somehow fitting—mute evidence of the ravages of time. Yet nothing could dim the magnificence of its contents.

On the main floor Jennifer paused in front of the statues of the Pharaoh Ramotet and his wife, sitting in state as they had more than five thousand years ago. It was hard to comprehend, but this serene, imperious couple had lived in 2660 B.C. Not only lived, but laughed and made love and suffered all the joys and sorrows that the human race is heir to. It was soothing, in a way—an affirmation of the continuity of time.

Drifting on, Jennifer inspected treasures great and small—magnificent limestone sarcophagi etched with detailed scenes of people performing everyday functions, great thronelike chairs that appeared to be made of pure gold, small translucent bowls as exquisite as teardrops, and tiny statues of stylized animals.

Pausing before a miniature reclining figure of an Egyptian girl holding a bowl shaped like a duck in her outstretched arms, Jennifer was entranced to discover that it had been used as a "cosmetic spoon." The delicate little whimsey, preserved through the ages, was proof that these people had indeed been human, with all the foibles and fancies of mankind.

Time passed unnoticed as Jennifer was transported

into the world of the Pharaohs. It was a voyage of enchanted discovery as she inspected their jewelry and their utensils, their statues and their gods. Hours went by and her mind was still not surfeited, but when her legs started to tremble with fatigue she realized that it was almost a full day since she had eaten. There was still so much to see, but it would never do to faint from hunger. Reluctantly, Jennifer decided she had better search for a restaurant.

There was a small cafe just a short distance away, and when she was shown to a table Jennifer sank down gratefully. After giving her order, she tried to slip back into the ambiance of ancient Egypt, but it was no good. The modern world kept intruding on all the thoughts she had held in abeyance for those enchanted hours inside the museum.

Kalim's giant shadow returned to hover over her like the wings of the great god Horus and she realized that he had never really left her thoughts, even while she drifted through the treasures of antiquity. There was one statue in particular that had reminded her of him—the same arrogant face with high cheekbones and penetrating dark eyes.

Jennifer gave a despairing sigh. Would there always be something to remind her of him? Broad shoulders towering over the crowd or a handsome aquiline profile barely glimpsed from a distance? She knew he had left an indelible mark on her life, but if she could only get far enough away from his disturbing presence, maybe the healing process would begin. If only she could go home!

That was the problem, but what was the solution? Unfortunately, at the moment she couldn't think of any. Pushing aside the half-eaten food, she stared at the tablecloth. What now? She couldn't very well wander around forever, but the idea of going back to the hotel was intolerable.

Walking aimlessly down the street after paying her bill, she saw a theater that advertised an American movie. It was an old film that she had seen years ago, but nostalgia filled her with a sudden yearning for anything that spoke of the safety of home. Besides, it was a haven and a postponement.

Slipping into a seat in the darkened theater, Jennifer stared at the screen as though it were a lifeline. The familiar accents fell softly on her ears and everything looked blessedly familiar—the clothes, the people, even the shaggy dog that played a small part. Gradually her tired body relaxed and it was only with great effort that she managed not to doze off. When the lights went on a long while later she blinked, returning reluctantly to reality.

It was dark when she trailed outside after the other patrons and, looking at her watch, Jennifer gasped at the time. It couldn't be that late! Of course she had gotten a very late start and spent hours and hours at the museum and then the movie, but still—

The crowd dissipated quickly, leaving Jennifer uncertain and alone, unwilling to leave the brightly lit space in front of the box office. Finally forcing herself to action, she wandered out to the sidewalk and was almost immediately surrounded by shadowy figures that appeared out of nowhere.

A sly dwarfish creature pulled at her skirt, begging for money, and an olive-skinned man with shifty eyes grasped her arm, offering to guide her through Cairo. His dirty fingernails scratched her soft skin and when she tried to pull away, he became more insistent. Other figures approached, hands outstretched, their voices more menacing than imploring.

Jennifer felt panic rising when, like a miracle, a cab stopped to discharge a man and woman in front of the theater. Bursting out of the circle around her, Jennifer made a dash for the taxi and scrambled inside before the man had even finished paying the driver. Slamming the door, she gave the name of the hotel and the car plunged off like a burro with a bee under its blanket.

The wild ride that followed had Jennifer clutching the seat with whitened knuckles. After the first near collision, she closed her eyes and was spared the driver's headlong maneuvers down narrow streets clogged with traffic. Loud imprecations and much horn blowing accompanied their progress, and although disaster seemed inevitable, they managed to arrive at the hotel a short, heart-stopping time later.

After the experiences she had been through, going up in the elevator was like going home, and as she walked down the corridor, Jennifer was enveloped by a blessed feeling of safety. It didn't last long.

Habeeb was standing like a guard outside Kalim's suite, and at first sight of her he disappeared inside. In a matter of moments Kalim erupted out of the room and confronted her so furiously that she took an involuntary step backward.

"Where have you been?" he demanded, seizing her arms and pinning them to her sides. She looked at him in surprise and opened her mouth, but before she could answer he shouted, "Do you know what time it is? Where were you?"

His fingers tightened cruelly, almost cutting off her circulation, and she winced. "You're hurting me."

Instead of releasing her, he increased the pressure until she almost cried out. His face darkened with rage as he said, "I ought to do more than that, you little idiot!"

At first, Jennifer had felt slightly guilty when she realized how long she had been gone. The premise of this trip was that she was here to do a job. Kalim was her boss, and even though the conference hadn't started yet, if there was any work to be done, she ought to be available to do it. But this treatment was completely uncalled for and her anger rose to meet his.

"I'm not accountable to you," she stormed. "I can go wherever I please!"

His punishing grip increased, threatening to leave bruises that would last for days, and his eyes were glacial slits as he hissed at her, "Where have you been?"

"I don't have to tell you," she said, defying him.

His hands fastened on her shoulders and he shook her so hard that her long silky hair tumbled over her face. "You will tell me—now!"

"I went to the Egyptian Museum," she muttered, frightened in spite of herself.

"That could not occupy you until this hour."

"Well, then I . . . I went to a movie." She couldn't quite meet his eyes, knowing that he was aware of her reason for postponing their meeting as long as possible.

"You went to a movie." The words were flat with disbelief. "And all this time I have been . . ." Breaking off, his eyebrows drew together in a scowl that formed two black lines. For a moment Jennifer was afraid that he was going to shake her again, but he controlled himself with an effort. "Do you know what could have happened to you on the streets of Cairo at night? Among other things, you could have been murdered for that silly little bauble you have around your neck."

Jennifer's fingers closed involuntarily around the jade pendant he had bought her in San Francisco and a stab of pain went through her. It was one of her cherished possessions, but to hear him describe it as a silly little bauble underscored his opinion of it—and her.

"Aren't you overstating things a bit?" she asked stiffly, unwilling to let him know how much it hurt.

The brunt of his anger seemed to have dissipated and

he gathered her long hair in both hands and used it to pull her head back so she had to look up at him. "What am I going to do with you, Jennifer?" he groaned. "Don't you know the danger you were in tonight?"

His palms cupped her face and almost absentmindedly he rubbed his thumbs gently back and forth across her jaw. Jennifer tried to ignore the warmth that stole through her and hung on desperately to her anger. Who did he think he was to shout at her like that and then caress her in that casual way and think that made everything all right?

Pulling away, she faced him coldly. "What I do doesn't concern you."

His face darkened and his mouth became a grim line. "That is a mistake on your part that I do not wish repeated. As long as you are in this country, you are subject to my rules. I will now spell them out for you. You will never"—he looked at her piercingly—"do you understand, *never*, go out unescorted after dark. At all other times you will inform me of your whereabouts. I do not wish to waste my time worrying about you or looking for you—is that clear?"

Jennifer's lips parted mutinously, but her long lashes fell before the adamant determination in his dark eyes. After surveying her downcast face for a moment, he smiled mirthlessly. "Good. I think we now understand each other. You will go to your room and stay there until I summon you."

By the time she looked up Kalim had disappeared into his suite, leaving her standing there like a small child who has been severely chastised. Feeling as though she had just been through a hurricane, Jennifer walked slowly down the corridor to her room.

A warm bath refreshed her tired body, but nothing could soothe her wounded feelings. The nerve of that insolent man! Who did he think he was to talk to her like that? If he had given her the slightest opening she would have told him exactly what he could do with his rules. But remembering the fury that had transfixed his handsome face, Jennifer had to acknowledge that she wouldn't have had the courage to do it.

After drying herself and putting on a robe, she realized that she was starving. The light lunch, only half eaten, was scarcely a memory now. Was part of her punishment being sent to bed without dinner? No, Kalim wouldn't do a childish thing like that, but he cared so little about her that he might not even think about it. Did she dare go down to the coffee shop in spite of his warning to stay in the room? A knock at the door solved her dilemma.

Jennifer was dressed in the same robe she had worn the night before and everything was so reminiscent of that harrowing experience that her whole body tensed in alarm. If Kalim thought he was going to do an instant replay, he was very much mistaken. This time she wouldn't even open the door.

"Who is it?" she called sharply.

To her relief, a foreign voice answered, "Room Service."

She opened the door to a smiling black-coated waiter, who wheeled in a table filled with silver-lidded dishes that gave forth delicious aromas. After positioning a straight-backed chair, he waited attentively to seat her and then bowed out of the room.

Rapidly removing the covers, Jennifer inspected a veritable feast and then began to eat with an appetite that did it justice. Pouring herself a second cup of coffee, her thoughts turned to Kalim. What a strange man he was. After reading her out like a marine top sergeant, he turned around and did a thoughtful thing like ordering her a magnificent dinner. Or did he order it himself? Most likely he just called downstairs and said, "Send something up to Miss Fairchild." Or had someone else do it.

It would be foolish to start ascribing any noble motives to him. Kalim was hard as nails. There wasn't a single chink in his armor, and if she started being grateful or trusting him even a little bit, it would be only strengthening his already powerful advantage.

Wandering over to the broad window, she curled up on the window seat and tucked her bare feet under her. Cairo was spread out like an animated canvas—a wicked, exciting, romantic city that was forbidden to her. In the distance she could see the enigmatic Sphinx and the wondrous Pyramids looming disproportionately large like statues in a primitive painting. The bright light that bathed them underlined their star billing in a city filled with major attractions.

Jennifer heaved a deep sigh. Was this as close as she would ever get to them? Had she come halfway around the world to view Egypt's mysteries through a pane of glass?

Chapter Five

Breakfast was delivered the next morning by a different waiter, this one in a white jacket, and Jennifer began to wonder bitterly if she were under house arrest.

After listlessly lifting the covers, she rejected the appetizing-looking dishes and settled for a piece of melon and some coffee. She was moodily pouring herself a second cup when there was a light tap at the door. Probably the waiter coming to collect the dishes. Carrying her cup with her, she went to tell him he could remove everything else. But it wasn't the waiter—it was Kalim.

Smiling at her surprised face, he walked in without waiting for an invitation. He was dressed casually in pale gray slacks and a matching silk shirt unbuttoned at the neck and Jennifer couldn't help staring at the strong column of his tanned throat.

Strolling over to the table, he viewed the untouched food with a frown. "Why didn't you eat your breakfast?"

"I had melon and coffee."

"That is not enough." Eyeing her slender figure, he said, "You are too thin."

Probably by his standards she was. Thinking of the

voluptuous Ayesha, Jennifer was annoyed at the unfavorable comparison. "Just chalk it up to one more way in which I fail to please you," she snapped.

With half-closed lids he surveyed her indolently. "Oh, I don't know. There are certain ways in which you please me very much."

Jennifer felt her face turn scarlet. "I wasn't talking about *that!*"

"It bothers you to talk about *that*, doesn't it?" he asked, mimicking her emphasis on the word.

His eyes were brimming with merriment and Jennifer was coldly furious. Why did it always turn out like this? He had a positive knack for putting her on the defensive, making her feel naive and unsophisticated.

While she was scrambling wildly in her mind for some suitably cutting remark, he threw back his head and laughed, white teeth gleaming against the deep tan of his face. "As I told you once before, you are a delight to tease, little one. But for today we shall call a truce because I have come to take you sight-seeing."

This abrupt change of mood from last night was startling and she looked at him warily. "Where are we going?"

"Anywhere you like. What do you wish to see?"

Jennifer hesitated for a moment, wanting to act disdainful, but the prospect he held out was just too enticing. The opportunity of seeing Cairo was irresistible.

"Oh, Kalim, do you really mean it?"

"Certainly. But we need not bother with the Egyptian Museum, since you have already seen that . . . thoroughly."

His mouth curved wryly, and for all his urbanity this morning, she knew he hadn't forgotten about last night. A certain hard purpose about him warned her not to repeat the performance, but she was too happy right now to care.

"Could we go to see the Sphinx and the Pyramids?"

"Of course. What would a trip to Egypt be without that? Dress in something cool and I will be back in one half hour."

The minute the door closed after him, Jennifer started scrambling into her clothes. Choosing a pale blue sleeveless linen dress with a white lace collar and a full skirt, she looked regretfully at a pair of spike-heeled white sandals and chose a low-heeled pair instead. This was no time for vanity. She was off on the sight-seeing trip of a lifetime and meant to make the most of it. Just as she was running a comb through her hair, Kalim arrived, and grabbing up her purse, she hurried to join him.

"Very nice," he said, surveying her approvingly. Draping a casual arm around her, he guided her out the door. She barely came up to his shoulder and, glancing down, he smiled. "I keep forgetting how tiny you are. 'Little one' is indeed the correct name for you."

She looked up from the circle of his hard, muscular arm and her cheek brushed his shoulder. Suddenly the casual embrace didn't seem as casual and she colored and moved away. There was a mocking gleam in his eye but he made no effort to detain her.

A car was waiting for them, and as it pulled away from the hotel Jennifer surveyed the sparkling Nile with increased wonder.

"It's beautiful but nothing like I imagined," she commented. "I never expected to see it meandering so peacefully past the city like this. Whenever I hear the name it always conjures up pictures of a wild river racing through vast steaming jungles with great big crocodiles slithering along the banks."

"Your visions are partially correct. The Nile comes to us from distant equatorial Africa where the waters do rush savagely and there are indeed crocodiles, crafty devils that often disguise themselves as logs in the river to await their unsuspecting prey."

It seemed impossible that this sun-kissed water, so placid between its tree-lined banks, could change character so drastically and Jennifer stared in fascination. The excitement of Cairo soon claimed her attention though as the car snaked in and out of narrow streets, some scarcely more than alleys.

"Is this the way to the Pyramids?"

He smiled at her absorbed face. She could hardly tear her eyes away from the window to ask the question. "I thought we would go to the Bazaar Khan el-Khalili first. I think you will enjoy seeing it. Shoppers have flocked there since the fourteenth century. There are still many wondrous things to be found but also many fakes made especially for the tourists." He shrugged. "I do not suppose it matters. They haggle, the shopkeeper makes a great show of anguish, the price is reduced, and everyone is happy. Bargaining is almost a national sport over here. You must do it or you cheat them of half the pleasure." He smiled at her. And then the smile faded. "But you will never come here alone."

Even though it reminded her of his autocratic prohibitions the night before, Jennifer couldn't work up any anger. Looking at the motley throng in the crowded smelly streets, she was very happy to have Kalim beside her.

Some of the people were obviously tourists. The omnipresent cameras slung around their necks were mute evidence along with the cumbersome over-the-shoulder flight bags. But they were outnumbered by the fellahin, the swarthy natives in their traditional galabias and skullcaps, and by the tall Nubians and the Bedouin, who bore the sharp features of the pure Arab.

"Would you like to walk for a while and look in the shops?" Kalim asked.

With a sense of déjà vu, Jennifer remembered how they had done the same thing in San Francisco. But there the resemblance ended—this was like a different world! As soon as the car door opened, they were immediately surrounded by a group of ragged children with outstretched palms, all shouting for baksheesh. Kalim distributed a handful of coins and then dispersed them with a few words. Jennifer noticed that a couple of tourists nearby were not so lucky. They were being besieged much as she had been last night, and at the memory she slipped her hand into Kalim's, unaware of the gesture.

His warm hand closed comfortingly over hers and he led her to a shop that displayed Egyptian pottery. Shallow uneven bowls and strange little statues with eyes deeply outlined in kohl crowded the window. To her untutored eye, they looked authentic, but reason told her that by their very profusion they were probably clever fakes mass-produced for the tourist trade. The door to the shop was curtained by long strings of colored glass beads and a slight breeze made them jangle together, adding to the cacophony around her.

"Do you wish to go in?" Kalim asked.

"I don't think so." She shook her head. "I just want to look."

He nodded and they strolled down the street, Kalim holding her hand and pausing obligingly whenever her attention was captured by a window display. Pottery gave way to the goldsmith section and Jennifer admired the exquisitely wrought jewelry and artifacts but still declined when Kalim wanted to take her inside for a closer inspection.

The exotic atmosphere was exciting, but after a while the heat and noise began to be oppressive. The odor of animal debris in the street mixed with the smell of overripe mangos, strong Arabic coffee, and the pungent aroma of spices, creating a curious mosaic for the nose. But when they passed an open-air butcher shop with an array of freshly butchered lambs on display, Jennifer turned to Kalim and said, "Could we get back in the car now?"

There was amused tolerance in his eyes. "Yes, I think it is time. We will go to see the Great Pyramid and your spirits will be soothed by its clean lines."

During the twenty-minute ride Kalim pointed out a few more sights along the way and Jennifer paid dutiful attention, but she was eager now to get to Giza.

Although she had viewed the Sphinx and the Pyramids from a distance, the close-up view was breathtaking. In spite of the crowds, the intrusive merchants, and the swarm of dragomen offering donkey and camel rides, these mysterious relics from the past were awe-inspiring. As Jennifer stood in the shadow of the Great Pyramid of Cheops and realized that it had been conceived more than 4,600 years ago, a great wonder filled her at the marvelous ingenuity of those ancient men.

As though guessing her thoughts, Kalim remarked, "Archaeologists have argued for many years about the method used for erecting these monuments. Especially since the pulley was unknown in Egypt before the Roman period. Some of these stone blocks weigh seven and a half tons. It was indeed a prodigious feat. Would you like to go inside?"

She nodded eagerly and he led her to the entrance. A scant half hour later she emerged slightly shaken. Although it was an experience she wouldn't have missed, Jennifer was glad to get outside once more. Reason should have warned her that since this was a tomb it would naturally feel constricted. But nothing had prepared her for the darkness and the stale air or the steep narrow ramps leading to a rabbit warren of connecting rooms. They must once have been magnificent when they were filled with golden treasure, but the low ceilings, sometimes only four feet in height, induced a claustrophobic feeling. And the thousands of tons of rock overhead were a sobering thought.

Emerging into the brilliant sunlight, Jennifer drew a deep breath of the hot dry air and Kalim regarded her understandingly. "I know. It is a somewhat frightening experience, but at least you can tell your friends at home that you were inside the tomb of the fabled Cheops." Snapping his fingers to an alert dragoman, Kalim said, "Now we will give you a different experience."

The man led a huge camel toward them and some money changed hands. Then, before Jennifer realized his intentions, Kalim lifted her onto the animal. Perched sidesaddle and looking down from a great height, she hung on desperately.

He laughed at the startled expression on her face and swung easily up behind her, putting his arms around her waist. "In deference to your skirt I did not put you astride, but do not worry, I will not let you fall."

The great beast turned his head and gave them a malevolent look, but the keeper tugged on the lead and with a swaying motion they lurched off across the sand.

With a gasp of delight Jennifer turned to Kalim. "This is another first for me."

His arms tightened and she could feel his hard chest against the curve of her breast. When he spoke, his mouth was so close that his warm breath tickled her ear. "I would like to provide all your firsts." She stiffened instinctively, but he drew her back with a low chuckle. "No, no, do not draw away from me, little one. We are having a truce, remember?"

"You're the one who broke it," she protested.

"Then I will stop. Nothing shall mar this day," he promised.

Relaxing in his arms, Jennifer felt a warmth steal

over her that had nothing to do with the strong sunlight. Looking up at him, she saw a wry smile on his lips and she smiled back.

"You're being so kind to me, Kalim. I don't know how to thank you. I know it can't be any fun for you doing all these tourist things."

"No, you are wrong. It is a long time since I have had so much . . . fun." One hand moved to her shoulder and slid caressingly up her neck. His long fingers traced the curve of her ear and Jennifer felt a sudden quickening of her pulses.

"Kalim, you promised!"

"So I did." He lifted her long hair and kissed the nape of her neck, his mouth warm and sensuous against her bare skin. A thrill quivered down her spine, but before she could protest, his arm dropped to her waist, holding her lightly. "And today I am your slave." His voice was very quiet as he added, "But tomorrow you may be mine."

Were the words teasing or threatening? Jennifer's sleeping distrust suddenly awoke. But they were riding by the Sphinx now and Kalim ordered the camel driver to halt. Confronted by the enigmatic man-headed lion, all other thoughts fled from her mind. With its face to the rising sun the great statue wore a serene look, as though it had solved all the mysteries of the universe.

"It is strange, is it not, that until nineteen twenty-six this same Sphinx was buried up to its neck in sand," Kalim told her.

"But that seems like such a short time ago!"

"Not even the flicker of an eyelash in its long history," he agreed.

"Is it as old as the Pyramids?"

"It dates back to the reign of Chephren, builder of the second pyramid," he said, indicating the smaller of the two structures.

"I suppose the weather was responsible for ruining the nose," Jennifer commented. "Was it sand storms through all these thousands of years?"

"That was the theory at one time. It was replaced by a more colorful explanation. A legend that refuses to die insists that the nose was destroyed by Napoleon's soldiers, who used it for target practice. Actually, it was done for religious reasons. As the dynasties rose and fell, Egypt was invaded by many people. At the time of the Arabs it was considered sacrilegious to represent the human face, so a Sufi named Saim-el-Dahr remedied the matter by disfiguring the nose."

"But surely it wasn't meant to be a man," she objected. "Isn't it supposed to be a rather fanciful statue of a lion?"

"Only partially. The head was carved in the likeness of the king, Chephren. The presence of a pleated headdress, a rampant cobra, and an Osiris beard completed the living image that fused king, lion, and man."

She looked at him in amazement. "How do you know all of this?"

"I could instruct you in much more than that," he said laughingly, dropping a light kiss on her temple. But when Jennifer made a face at him, he answered her question matter-of-factly. "In my part of the world, ancient history is very real and we study it from an early age. Count your blessings." He gave her an impish grin. "I could have bored you with a mountain of memorized facts and figures."

Before she could comment, their driver resumed the tour and the great beast was once more lumbering across the sand. It moved with a peculiar swaying motion, and for some time Jennifer had been aware of a feeling that was almost like seasickness.

"Kalim," she said hesitantly, "I've enjoyed the ride, but do you think we could get off now?"

96

He threw back his head and laughed in an uninhibited way. "I was wondering how long it would take. Camel riding is an acquired taste, but you did very well for your first time."

A word to the dragoman stopped the animal and Kalim jumped down agilely, holding up his arms to Jennifer. His strong hands spanned her waist and she put her arms around his neck to be lowered to the ground. As she slid along his length, Jennifer was aware of the hard flatness of his body and the fact that he was deliberately holding her close.

The magnetism between them was instantly ignited and the noise of the surrounding people disappeared. Over Kalim's shoulder she could see the brooding Pyramids and the timeless Sphinx, watching them with an indecipherable smile on its ruined face. The sun burned in a cloudless blue sky and Jennifer was transported four thousand years backward into time. Did Chephren bring his queen here to view his masterpiece? And did he hold her in his arms while her heart swelled with love for his wondrous accomplishment?

Kalim's soft voice brought her back to the present. "As much as I am enjoying this, I think it is time for your next first."

For a moment she stared at him in a daze, reluctant to return to reality. Then, realizing that she still had her arms around his neck, she blushed furiously and moved away. "What . . . I mean, where are we going?"

"Allow me to surprise you," he said with a smile.

He guided her to the waiting car and she sank gratefully against the soft seat, the welcome air conditioning cooling her flushed cheeks.

On the road back to Cairo Kalim kept up a steady flow of conversation and Jennifer was grateful, realizing that he was trying to spare her any embarrassment she might have felt over that illusive moment in Giza. What a strange, complex man he was. How could he be so autocratic one moment and so gentle and understanding the next? Would she ever understand him?

They were entering the outskirts of Cairo, and after a short time the car pulled over to the curb. A green and white canopy extended from an ornately carved lintel to the edge of the sidewalk, but since the lettering on the window was in Arabic, Jennifer had no idea where they were.

"What is this place?" she asked.

"It is called Ahotep. We will have lunch here. We have had food for the soul, now we shall have nourishment for the body."

She had been too absorbed to think about eating, but as she followed Kalim into the restaurant Jennifer realized that she was hungry.

The doorway was curtained with the long strands of beads so commonplace in Cairo and he held them aside for her to enter a large, dimly lit room. It was cool after the glare outside and big ceiling fans made a soothing sound as they circled lazily overhead. Upholstered couches lined the walls and in front of each was a low wooden table exquisitely inlaid in mother-of-pearl. Thick squashy cushions sat on the floor and there were a few groups occupying them, but Kalim led her to one of the sofas.

"I hope you do not mind eating with your fingers." She looked to see if he were joking, but his twinkling eyes gave her no clue.

Before she could question him, a handsome Egyptian youth wearing a brown galabia patterned in orange approached their table. He carried a large basin under one arm and a graceful etched brass pitcher in his hand.

The basin was deposited in the middle of the table and Kalim said, "Stretch out your hands—no, no, palms up."

Totally mystified, Jennifer did as she was told. Kalim stretched his hands next to hers and to her astonishment the waiter poured steaming, scented water over them.

"*Voilà!* Now that we have washed our hands like good little children, we can have our lunch," Kalim said, laughing at the look on her face as the waiter handed them each a thick towel.

No menus were presented and they weren't asked for their order. The first course just appeared. It looked like a stew made of tomatoes and celery and some delicious-smelling spices, but there was no silverware. Jennifer wondered if it would be polite to mention the fact or just wait until Kalim noticed it for himself, but before she had made up her mind, the waiter reappeared with a huge cone-shaped straw basket filled with chunks of coarse white bread.

When she refused politely, Kalim said, "It is best that you take some."

Watching in surprise, she soon understood his advice as he dipped the bread in his plate and maneuvered a piece of tomato onto it with a well-manicured forefinger.

"Do not look so startled, my little Yankee—it is done in the very best society."

Well, when in Rome, Jennifer thought, and dug in with a will. The food was delicious and she was very hungry.

The rest of the meal was equally bizarre. There was soup, which posed no problem since it could be drunk directly from the cup. Then a large brass tray appeared with delicate little birds that Kalim told her were pigeons. Accompanying them was a concoction made of broad noodles and bits of chicken, among other things, all dusted over with cinnamon and sugar and looking something like a round coffee cake. By this time Jennifer thought nothing of reaching over to break off a piece with her fingers and even offered to do the same for Kalim.

Finally she leaned back against the cushions and said, "It was divine, but I can't eat another bite. In fact, I don't think I'll be able to eat for days!"

"I am happy that you have enjoyed our food." His eyes were enigmatic as they contemplated her. "Perhaps I shall make a convert of you yet."

She smiled up at him gratefully. "If every day could be as wonderful as this one has been, perhaps you could."

He took her hand and his thumb made a slow circle on the soft skin of her inner wrist. "And if I could make that promise?" he asked softly. Jennifer felt a warning thrill invade her and she pulled her hand away. Kalim let it go without a struggle, making her feel slightly foolish about her instinctive gesture. "Now we shall have our tea," he said easily.

He clapped his hands together and a young boy approached carrying a tray with two tall glasses, the bottom of each encased in a little straw jacket. Then their waiter appeared bearing a beautifully engraved brass teapot with a long spout like a watering can. To Jennifer's complete amazement, he held the pot high above his head and poured the fragrant tea into the waiting glasses without spilling a drop. Kalim burst into laughter at the look on her face.

"How on earth does he do that?" she asked.

"It takes a great deal of practice, and much spilled tea, before one becomes an expert."

"I can certainly believe that!"

The tea was strong, hot, and minty, a pleasant end to a sumptuous meal. Jennifer leaned back with a satisfied sigh. "When I get back home this will all seem like a dream and I'll bet there will be times when even I don't believe it."

"Do you miss your home very much?"

"I haven't been gone long enough," she said with a laugh.

"But suppose you were," he insisted. "What then? Could you live happily outside your own country?"

"I can't envision any possibility of that."

"What if circumstances arose that made it necessary?"

She looked at him warily. "Are you by any chance offering me a permanent job?"

"No, the question was merely hypothetical," he said. "I was trying to understand your people better. I have lived many places and have known many cultures, but Americans are foreign to me. They do not seem to leave their own country except as tourists."

She gave him a gamin grin. "Well, you can't complain on that score. We've inundated the world in recent years."

"But only as visitors who go back home as predictably as lemmings."

"Isn't that natural?" she asked.

"Not necessarily. I, for instance, was born in Egypt, educated in England, and spent my holidays in Europe. I can be comfortable living in many places. Could you?" He looked at her sharply.

"I don't know," she said slowly. "I've traveled so little that I'd probably jump at any chance, but if I couldn't go home . . ." She considered the question gravely. "I guess there would have to be a very compelling reason for keeping me there."

He looked at her contemplatively, but before he could comment the young boy who had brought the tea glasses approached. "Your pardon, sir, but are you Mr. Kalim Al Kahira?" At Kalim's nod he said, "A message for you, sir, from your hotel. You are wanted there."

A shadow of annoyance darkened Kalim's face momentarily and then he shrugged. "It is sad, but pleasure must give way to business."

Jennifer looked at her watch and was scandalized!

"We've been gone almost all day," she gasped. "I shouldn't have kept you so long."

"You did not keep me." His warm hand covered hers, lying on the table. "It was my idea, remember? And as I recall, I had to convince you. Perhaps next time you will not give me so much trouble."

His reference to the tangled relations between them embarrassed her, but she put it out of her mind. It had been a wonderful day and Kalim had been so kind to her.

"I can't thank you enough for today," she said simply. "You have so many friends in Cairo, besides your business here, and I appreciate your giving me so much time."

"Perhaps I was trying to cement relations between our two countries," he said lightly.

"If that was your purpose, you certainly succeeded," she replied. "I'm in love with your city."

"This is not, strictly speaking, my city. I have factories here, but my home is in Luxor."

"Well, I'm sure I should fall in love with that also," she assured him. Although the words were an automatic polite response, Jennifer suddenly realized they were true. "This part of the world is different from anything I've ever known. It's like living in a storybook with an adventure around every corner. I wish I could see every bit of it."

His eyes were opaque as he studied her face. "Perhaps you shall. On our next excursion I shall take you to El Faiyûm. It is a beautiful oasis in the desert. And we shall visit the ruins of the Crocodilopolis. Would you like that?"

"It sounds fascinating." Her eyes shone. "I know it has something to do with crocodiles, but what?"

"It is where the water god Sebek was worshipped. The lake by the temple was once filled with sacred crocodiles wearing jeweled bands around their legs and necks. They were fed sacrificial offerings and came promptly when the priests called to them by name."

Jennifer shivered. "I'm not going to ask what those offerings were."

"You are wise," he said. "Everything in life does not benefit by being reduced to words."

Their waiter stood at Kalim's elbow with the check and Jennifer sighed, wishing the day didn't have to end. But Kalim had someone waiting to see him. Something suddenly occurred to her. "How did they know to reach you here?"

"This is one of my, how do you say—haunts. Whoever is looking for me probably left messages throughout the city."

"I do hope you didn't miss anything important," Jennifer said worriedly.

He took her hand and raised it to his lips. "I did not miss anything today," he said quietly.

Jennifer knew that his polite remark was just an example of continental manners, the kind of thing an experienced man said to his date as a matter of course. That included kissing her hand. He wouldn't expect her to be naive enough to think it meant anything. But as she preceded him out of the restaurant, her heart was singing.

Chapter Six

They had scarcely entered the lobby of the hotel before Ayesha detached herself from a group and came sauntering over. Jennifer wondered bitterly what kind of radar enabled her to keep turning up like a bad penny. This time she was due for a disappointment though, since Kalim had business waiting. That was some consolation.

Ayesha's dark eyes held an ominous glitter as they rested on Jennifer, but her expression changed when she faced Kalim. "It is about time you returned," she said, pouting. "I left messages everywhere."

"That was you?" For a moment, a frown drew Kalim's eyebrows together. "What is wrong?"

Ayesha looked up seductively from under her long eyelashes. "I missed you. You have been gone an eternity."

Kalim looked at her incredulously. "You *missed* me and that is why you sent a message that I was wanted at the hotel?"

"It is true, is it not?" Ayesha hugged his arm to her side, curling herself so sinuously around him that Jennifer half expected to hear her purr. The long red nails smoothing his lapel were indeed reminiscent of claws.

Kalim's laugh rang out in the lobby. "What shall I do with you, Ayesha?" he asked, shaking his head helplessly. "As I have told you many times, you are a spoiled child, but one of these days you will get your comeuppance. What will happen, I wonder, when you find you cannot get your own way?"

"That day will never come," she told him confidently.

They were joined by the friends Ayesha had been chatting with and Jennifer automatically stepped out of the charmed circle, knowing she didn't belong there.

"René has chartered a boat and we are going to cruise down the Nile, perhaps all the way to Beni Suef," Ayesha told him. "That is why I was so impatient for you to return. We wish to start soon."

Kalim's smile cushioned his refusal. "Not this evening, chérie. I have work to do."

"Work? That is just nonsense!"

"Perhaps to you," he conceded, "but we cannot all frolic in the sunshine."

"There will be moonlight tonight," she offered seductively.

Kalim merely laughed and shook his head, but Ayesha continued to wheedle. When she finally realized that he might actually mean it, her voice took on an acid edge.

"If you had not been wasting your time all day . . ." But the words trailed off at the ominous look on his face.

Other voices chimed in urging him to reconsider and Jennifer turned away. It was midnight for Cinderella and her party was over. Kalim had forgotten her existence as he always did when his own world formed a protective layer around him.

Walking slowly toward the elevator, she pondered over this contradictory man. There were so many demands on his time—why had he given her this wonderful day? Was it guilt over his treatment last night—or the night before? Or was it pity? Did he know that just being with him affected her like a strong cocktail? Jennifer's cheeks burned at the thought that her emotions were as naked as her body had been. Maybe he was just being kind to her like an older man to a teenager with a crush. The idea was odious and her fingernails bit into her clenched palms.

Fleeing into a waiting elevator, she had a last glimpse of Kalim surrounded by people, all trying to capture his attention. Everyone wanted to be with him—at least she wasn't alone in that. But what made her think she could possibly compete?

There was only one other person in the elevator and Jennifer barely glanced at him as she gave her floor number to the operator.

But as the doors slid shut, her fellow passenger said, "Excuse me, but you're American, aren't you?"

Turning, she saw a tall, thin young man with light brown hair and a pleasant, open face. "Yes, I am," she admitted, "how did you guess?"

He grinned at her. "It takes one to know one." He held out his hand. "My name is John Belmont and I'm very proud to make your acquaintance, ma'am."

His eager, unsophisticated manner was disarming and, taking the proffered hand, she smiled at him. "You're from the South, aren't you?"

The elevator made a series of stops and they moved to the back of the car. "That's right—Louisiana," he said in the soft drawl that had given him away. "I'm the assistant curator at the museum in New Orleans and, unlike you lucky tourists, I'm here working."

Jennifer's mouth twisted wryly at the thought of

herself as a carefree tourist. If he only knew! But the elevator had reached her floor and she merely said, "Well, it was nice meeting you, John. I get off here."

After edging her way out, she saw that he was right behind her. "Is this your floor too?" she asked, surprised at the coincidence.

"Not really," he admitted, "but I couldn't just let you disappear." At the look on her face he said, "Please don't get me wrong. I'm not trying to pick you up."

"It looks remarkably like it," she commented coolly. "Even in Cairo some things are the same."

"You're wrong about that. *Nothing* is the same here. I'm about a million miles from home and you're the first friendly face I've seen. Couldn't you please stay and talk to me for a minute? I'm so doggone lonesome I could howl at the moon."

He did look rather desperate and Jennifer took pity on him and stopped walking down the hall. "But if you're working here, surely you've met some people?"

"A few. But after work they go their way and I go mine. Mostly I just wander around hoping to hear some English spoken. I never knew there were so many other languages in the world!" Jennifer eyed him sympathetically and he blurted out, "Would you have dinner with me tonight?" Before she could refuse, he hurried on, "I can have the American Embassy vouch for me and I'll show you my driver's license and even my library card."

Her lips twitched. "What would that prove except that you're an American who drives a car and knows how to read?"

"What if I showed you a picture of my mother and my two sisters?" he asked hopefully.

"That won't be necessary." Jennifer laughed. "To tell you the truth, you look very nice, and I think I

107

might have accepted if I hadn't just finished a huge lunch."

"But it's early yet. These people don't eat dinner until all hours." She could tell he considered that another black mark against the country. "If you're traveling with a friend—if that's what's bothering you—I'd be glad to take both of you," he persisted.

Jennifer thought of Kalim. By no stretch of the imagination could he be considered a friend. Her soft mouth tightened as she recalled the way Ayesha had reclaimed her property. Any thought of Jennifer had been completely driven out of his mind, and after the brunette bombshell worked her wiles on him, they would be cruising down the Nile, watching the romantic pattern of moonbeams on the water. Kalim would have his arm around Ayesha's waist and his lips would look for that special place behind her ear . . .

"I'd be happy to have dinner with you tonight," Jennifer told John abruptly.

Although bewildered by this sudden switch, he took her up on it with alacrity. After arranging to meet in the lobby at nine o'clock, John got back on the elevator and Jennifer walked down the corridor to her room, a determined tilt to her chin. A short time later the telephone rang.

"Why did you run away?" Kalim's impatient voice in her ear demanded.

"I didn't think you noticed," she told him stiffly.

There was smothered annoyance in his voice. "Of course I noticed. I am asking why you disappeared."

"What difference does it make? You did your good deed for today."

There was a short silence and then Kalim said ominously, "Come to my suite."

"I'd rather not."

His voice was silky, but this time there was no

mistaking the steel. "I do not think you understand. I am not asking you—I am ordering you."

"And if I refuse?" But it was sheer bravado, as her knees were shaking. She knew to her sorrow that Kalim in a rage was awesome.

"I think you would regret that decision."

"Oh, all right," Jennifer muttered, giving in unwillingly.

As she walked down the hall every nerve was on red alert. Facing him a few minutes later, she knew her apprehension was justified. Where was the charming companion of this afternoon? Kalim lounged in an armchair like a king giving audience to a particularly troublesome peasant. His dark eyes surveyed her coolly.

"I must confess you baffle me, Jennifer. I thought we had an enjoyable day."

His phrasing grated on her raw nerves. Was that all it was to him—"an enjoyable day"? Well, what did she expect? But did that include the camel ride? Jennifer grew weak as she remembered his strong arms supporting her in the saddle and the way he had gently lifted her long hair and kissed that vulnerable spot on the nape of her neck. That was an inspired improvisation, an extra something thrown in to keep the poor little American waif happy—and it had worked. A tingle went down her spine even now as she relived the moment.

Today had been the most wonderful day of her life, but if she needed any proof that it hadn't meant anything to him, it was provided by his attitude toward Ayesha. When he found out it was she who summoned him back, he wasn't annoyed, merely amused. Perhaps he was relieved that she had given him a graceful exit. Was it possible they had even *prearranged* it? Jennifer crossed her arms and gripped her elbows to keep in the hurt.

"Did you or did you not have a good time today?" he asked, impatient in the face of her silence.

Jennifer called up all her reserves. She would die sooner than let him know how devastated she was! "It was very nice," she managed to say in a cool little voice, "and I believe I thanked you for it."

His face darkened with anger and he stood up abruptly, looming very large above her. "You know what you can do with your thanks!"

"Would you like me to kneel down and touch my forehead to the floor or would a simple curtsy suffice?" she asked sarcastically.

His fingers bit into her shoulders with such strength that Jennifer winced with pain, but she bit her lower lip, refusing to give him the satisfaction of crying out.

"That acid tongue of yours will buy you more trouble one day than you anticipate," he told her through clenched teeth. "It is a good thing that you are a woman."

"And if I were a man what would you do? Knock me down?" She flung out the challenge defiantly.

He looked at her contemptuously. "Did I call you a woman? Let me amend that. You are more of a child than Ayesha."

The comparison to her hated rival enraged Jennifer and she erupted, the words fairly tumbling out. "Even as a child I had more manners than your precious friend. In *my* country she would be considered down-right rude!"

His hands loosened their punishing grip and comprehension dawned, chasing away the anger. "So that's it," he murmured softly.

Too late she realized that he thought she was jealous of Ayesha. The evidence was written plainly on his face and it infuriated her. "No, that's *not* it!" she raged impotently. "I'm well aware that you consider yourself

110

irresistible to all women, but I wouldn't have you on a silver platter with an apple in your mouth!"

A mocking smile twisted his finely chiseled lips and he regarded her through half-closed lids. "Are you sure?"

His hands clasped her slender waist, drawing her slowly closer, and Jennifer felt her panic rising. She knew from bitter experience how Kalim could arouse her senses and was determined not to let it happen again. If she responded in the slightest way her self-respect would be gone forever. It was a game to him and he was just playing with her.

Sliding his hands tantalizingly across her back, he bent his dark head toward her while she struggled desperately. "No, Kalim, don't! I don't want you to."

He held her easily and there was a mocking look on his face. "Kiss me and then I will know if you are telling the truth."

His tone was sensuous, inviting her into his web, and in spite of everything she wanted to enter. How could his slightest touch set off such a fire in her blood? It took a tremendous will to resist those warm hands that seemed to burn right through to her bare body. It would be so easy to relax in his arms and let him teach her to love. Even as the traitorous thought entered her mind, Jennifer realized the danger and stiffened in his arms, but his strength easily overcame her pitiful efforts.

Drawing her closer until she could feel the length of his body pressing against hers, he brushed his lips against her cheek. When she turned her head, his mouth found hers and she was lost. Kalim's sure hands caressed her body expertly while his mouth teased the corners of hers until her lips parted helplessly. As he outlined their delicate shape with his tongue, Jennifer felt a wild desire that started in her lower limbs and spread throughout her whole body. With a despairing moan she twisted her head aside but Kalim kissed her throat and when his warm mouth slid over her heated skin the flames leaped higher.

Jennifer was lost and she knew it, but as she felt the last barrier being torn away, her glazed eyes focused on a glass of water on the table next to them. In desperation she seized it and poured it down the back of Kalim's neck.

With a muttered oath, he released her, and Jennifer ran to the door. But before she could turn the knob, his voice rang out, stopping her in her tracks.

"Jennifer!" The authoritative tone rooted her to the spot and she stood with her back to him, powerless to move. "Turn around." Unwillingly, she did as she was told. He walked slowly toward her and she remained motionless, staring at the carpet. "Look at me." Raising mutinous green eyes, she waited for the storm to break, but Kalim's face was impassive. "That was a very foolish thing you did and you shall pay for it. You know that, don't you?" The very absence of anger in his expressionless voice made him all the more dangerous and Jennifer started to tremble. "You are a little hellcat and I am going to enjoy taming you. Like all cats you will resist, but when I have finished, you will come to me at the snap of my fingers."

There was a cruel smile on his dark face and Jennifer looked at him in a kind of horror. At that moment, she had no doubt that he meant to destroy her will—one way or another. The knowledge was terrifying. With a smothered cry, she tore her eyes away from him and ran from the room.

Throwing herself face down on her bed a few moments later, Jennifer waited for her wildly racing heart to slow down. What had possessed her to do such a rash thing? Kalim was unpredictable at all times, but now she had made him an implacable enemy. What had happened was his own fault, of course, but that wouldn't help any. Did he actually have plans for retribution or was that only a threat to frighten her? If that were the case, he would be delighted to know how well he had succeeded!

As the minutes ticked by, Jennifer's mind searched wildly for a way to escape from this cruel, despotic man, but the situation hadn't changed. Now more than ever he would hang on grimly to her passport, and without it she was in his power. Where did he keep it? She raised her head, eyes wide with speculation. Perhaps she could search his room! But even as the wild hope surfaced, it died a quick death. It could be anywhere, and if Kalim caught her—or worse yet, Habeeb . . . Jennifer shuddered at the thought.

Pounding the pillow with small clenched fists, she gritted her teeth in frustration. Why hadn't she followed her instincts and refused to part with the precious thing? But it was foolish to indulge in futile regrets. Next time she would know better—assuming she got out of this present mess.

Gradually the events of the chaotic day began to take their toll and her eyelashes drooped against her flushed cheeks. A great weariness claimed her mind and body, and after a while Jennifer slept.

When she awoke the room was in darkness and for a moment her confused mind thought she was in her apartment in San Francisco. Then her memory came crowding back, reminding her, among other things, that she had a date with John Belmont. Suddenly the prospect was very appealing. What time was it? Glancing hurriedly at her watch, she saw that there was still plenty of time.

With arms crossed behind her head, Jennifer thought about the man she had met so casually in the elevator. She would never have done a thing like that at home, but the circumstances were different here. Jennifer could understand his desperate need to be with a fellow American because at the moment she felt that way herself. It would be nice to be with a plain ordinary man for a change, someone she could understand. John didn't look like the reincarnation of one of the ancient pagan gods and his ingenuous eyes wouldn't have the power to see into her very soul. If he put his hand on her arm, it wouldn't set off a fire in her blood . . .

Abruptly, Jennifer jumped off the bed and went into the bathroom to turn on the shower. Tonight was going to be fun and she wasn't going to let Kalim spoil it. Stepping into the tiled shower, she raised her face resolutely to the stinging spray.

After blow drying her hair to a fluffy golden cloud, she selected a simple outfit that the saleslady had assured her would be suitable for any occasion. The outfit consisted of a slim white silk ottoman skirt and a black silk knit top, the wide scooped neckline and short sleeves of which were edged in the same white silk as the skirt. Looking in the mirror, Jennifer decided that she looked quite sophisticated and was annoyed with herself for experiencing a moment's regret that Kalim wouldn't see her in it. Hadn't she vowed not to think about him tonight?

The lobby disclosed an incredible hub of boiling activity when the elevator doors opened on the ground floor. A tour must have just arrived because the beautiful mosaic floor was completely covered with mountains of expensive luggage and hundreds of chattering, excited people. The din mounted as they called back and forth to each other and milled around the big room. It was impossible for the clerks to take care of them all at once, but that didn't seem to bother the vacationers. They made plans and visited with each other as though they hadn't just traveled thousands of miles on the same plane.

Jennifer despaired of ever finding John in the mob scene, but her fears were groundless. He was waiting by the elevator bank and his eyes lit up when he saw her. "You look fantastic."

"Thank you," she said, smiling. "I wasn't sure we'd ever get together in this crowd. What's going on?"

"Two big tours just came in. One from Australia and one from the United States."

She grinned at him. "How lucky can you get! You were dying to hear English spoken and now you have an embarrassment of riches. Perhaps we should stay right here so you can make some contacts."

"I already hit the jackpot, so let's get out of this madhouse." He turned her toward the entrance and they began to pick their way cautiously through the crowd.

Halfway to the door, Jennifer turned to make a laughing comment and found herself looking straight into Kalim's narrowed black eyes. They were separated by scores of people, but she was held as if by a magnet. His expression was formidable and she hesitated, remembering the rules he had laid down. Always tell him where she was going and never go out alone at night. Well, she wasn't alone. But should she have told him about her date with John? Maybe she ought to introduce them and explain. The last thing she wanted to do was provoke Kalim further.

As she paused irresolutely, Ayesha came up behind him. Standing on tiptoes, she put her hands kittenishly over Kalim's eyes. Jennifer felt raw anger course through her, and without waiting to see Kalim's happy look of surprise, she pushed her way ruthlessly through the crowd.

"The New Orleans Saints could sure use you," John drawled admiringly. "It would have taken me twice as long to get us through that mess."

Jennifer smiled ruefully. "I guess I could have been penalized for unnecessary roughness, but I suddenly felt the urgent need for a breath of fresh air."

They went to a restaurant called Charlie's American Grill. It had a long polished bar the length of the room and the dining area was furnished with leather booths. A refrigerated glass case near the entry displayed thick steaks with pats of butter on top carved in the shape of roses.

John looked around the dimly lit room with satisfaction. "I discovered this place about a week ago. It's the only restaurant I know of here where you can get a decent steak. I figured you'd like it after all that crazy foreign food."

They could very easily have been in a restaurant anywhere in the United States and Jennifer's smile was a little fixed as she remembered the charming luncheon at the Ahotep that afternoon. But that was all over and done with. Making a special effort, she said, "It looks very nice."

He asked if steak and French fries sounded all right and she nodded, since the most exotic item on the menu was fried prawns. She did venture to ask him though if he had sampled any of the local cuisine.

"Oh, I tried it when I first got here, but it didn't agree with me. And I think all that hocus-pocus with the tea is downright silly."

Jennifer carefully straightened her fork and changed the subject. "Tell me about your work."

John was transformed into a different person when he talked about the Museum. The critical, condescending attitude was replaced with genuine enthusiasm. Although it was obvious that he was too homesick to appreciate modern Egypt, he was clearly in love with her antiquities. And very knowledgeable about them, too.

116

Jennifer told him of her visit to the Egyptian Museum. "I wish I had known you then. There were so many questions I'd like to have asked."

"I'll give you a guided tour," he promised. "I'm sure you want to go back."

"Oh, yes—it's impossible to see everything in one day."

"I know what you mean. Overwhelming, isn't it? And that's only the tip of the iceberg. You wouldn't believe the priceless things they have just stored any which way in back rooms. My job is to persuade them to loan us some. Nothing on the scale of the King Tut exhibit, of course—just enough of a collection to round out an Egyptian wing we're trying to put together."

"That shouldn't present much of a problem."

"You wouldn't think so. They'd never even miss the few things we're requesting. But the amount of red tape involved is incredible. There's no telling how long I'm going to be stuck here."

"But as a curator you must really appreciate the opportunity to spend so much time inspecting the exhibits. I was fascinated and I didn't even know what I was looking at. There was one item, for instance . . ." And she described the exquisite cosmetic bowl held by the delicate figure of a young girl.

"Those are a big hit with the ladies," he said, smiling. "It comes as a shock to realize that over three thousand years ago cosmetics were used in much the same way as they are today. Ancient Egyptian women used pigments to tint their faces and even applied lip rouge with a brush as you probably do. They plucked their eyebrows, dyed their hair, and painted their finger- and toenails. The only thing that's changed is that men in those days used cosmetics, too. They also wore jewelry."

"They still do that," Jennifer pointed out.

"Not like then. The necklaces and bracelets those fellows decked themselves out in were more elaborate than the ladies'."

"Then some of those magnificent ornaments I saw could have belonged to men," she exclaimed. "That explains it. There was one necklace I fell in love with, but it looked so heavy I didn't see how a woman could wear it and still hold her head up. It was a gold collar fashioned like the wings of a huge bird and it was all inlaid with red and blue and green stones."

"The bird might have been a depiction of Nekhebet, the vulture, or the Horus, the falcon, and the gems were undoubtedly carnelian, turquoise, and lapis lazuli. Those were their precious stones. Turquoise was mined in the Sinai, but lapis was especially expensive because it had to be imported from Afghanistan, an arduous journey in those days."

He went on to tell fascinating stories about ancient gods and strange ritualistic customs and the evening passed quickly. When Jennifer noticed that the restaurant was almost empty, she couldn't believe how long they had been sitting there.

"It looks like they're getting ready to close," she remarked, glancing around. "It's been a wonderful evening, John, I don't know where the time has gone."

"I hope I haven't bored you silly," he said anxiously. "When I get started I'm afraid there's no stopping me."

"I enjoyed every minute of it, really I did," she assured him.

"Good—then you'll go out with me again?"

"I'd be happy to," she replied.

After the waiter had taken the check, John said, "Would you like to stop at the Hilton for an after-dinner drink? It's just like back home and at least you don't have to worry about the water there."

Jennifer felt a curious letdown. John had been such a sparkling companion during dinner that she had almost forgotten his curious bias against anyplace that wasn't the United States. Wasn't it strange? If things had been different she would have gloried in the opportunity to see Egypt. And even under the circumstances there was an excitement about just being here that gripped her every time she looked at the Nile flowing beneath her window or glimpsed an onion-domed mosque with its patina of antiquity. There were probably a lot of people like John, though. Too bad—they didn't know what they were missing.

After hailing a taxi outside of the restaurant he said, "I'm afraid I've monopolized the conversation. I promise to let you do the talking for the rest of the evening."

But she shook her head. "Next time. It's getting late and I really have to get back."

He attempted to change her mind, but when Jennifer convinced him that she didn't want a drink, he took her back to the hotel.

Actually, she was beginning to feel slightly nervous. Her anger at the beginning of the evening had dissipated and the threat of an irate Kalim was hanging over her. It had been foolish to turn her back on him in the lobby—foolish and dangerous. Why was she always provoking him, adding fuel to the fire? Even granted that she had acted childishly, though, what was there to worry about? She was a free agent and entitled to go out with whomever she pleased. Kalim only had a right to her working hours.

But walking softly down the broad hallway after saying good night to John, Jennifer cast an apprehensive glance at his closed door. Would he come charging out again to subject her to another torrent of abuse? The door remained shut, but it wasn't until she was safely inside her own room that she breathed a sigh of relief. The fact that it was slightly tinged with regret made her furious. She had to be out of her mind to want another encounter with that Satan! Besides, he probably wasn't even back yet. He and the sultry Ayesha must be out painting the town. Since she had given up her boat trip to be with him, he was undoubtedly making it up to her.

Flinging her purse down angrily, Jennifer started to get ready for bed.

Chapter Seven

Jennifer got up early the next morning as a matter of habit, but she wondered listlessly what she would do with herself all day. Yesterday at this time there had been a knock at the door that had heralded adventure. Kalim had invited her out for a day that would live in her memory forever. Was it only yesterday? How had things gone so wrong between them again in such a short time? It was unlikely that he would ever want to repeat the offer.

The shrilling telephone brought a sudden wild hope to her heart, but when she answered it that hope died quickly.

"I wish to see you in my suite," Kalim's cold voice announced.

She had put on jeans and a pale blue T-shirt that molded her soft curves closely. Looking at herself now, she debated the advisability of changing to something more suitable and then decided against it. Let his fancy girl friend wear the seductive gowns. Ayesha's hips were too big for jeans anyway, Jennifer thought spitefully.

Entering Kalim's suite a moment later, she shoved

both hands into her back pockets and faced him defiantly. "You wanted to see me?"

A small smile twitched the corners of his mouth as he surveyed her and then it was gone. His voice was cold as he asked, "Who was that you were with last night?"

"I don't think that concerns you," she said, but at the look in his eyes, she added reluctantly, "A friend—he's an American."

"And where did you meet this . . . friend?"

"What difference does it make?" As he continued to look at her, the words were forced out. "I met him here in the hotel."

"You met a stranger in the hotel and you went out with him just like that?" He snapped his fingers.

"It wasn't like that," she muttered, furious because that's exactly the way it looked even though there were extenuating circumstances. Why did everything she did give Kalim the wrong impression?

"Perhaps you will tell me exactly how it was," he said, a thin line of steel under the courteous words.

"Well, he's . . . he's an American," she blurted out.

Kalim shook his head. "Jennifer, you are how old—twenty-two? I wonder how you have existed this long without a keeper."

His patronage infuriated her. "I am perfectly capable of taking care of myself and I wish you would stop treating me like a feeble-minded child!"

"Perhaps I will when you stop acting like one."

"I don't see what I did that was so wrong," she cried.

"Accepting an invitation from a strange man may not be wrong in your country, but I am sure it is considered risky even there."

"For your information, John was a perfect gentleman!"

"And you could tell that he would be just by looking at him?"

"Well . . . yes," she said defensively. Kalim's male

look of derision made her temper flare and without counting the consequences she said hotly, "Of course, sometimes appearances are deceiving."

A mask descended over his face. "I presume that was directed at me." She bit her lip and turned to go but his voice was like a whip. "Miss Fairchild! In case it has slipped your mind, I *am* your employer and I believe it is time I started getting something for my money." He went to the table by the window and picked up a sheaf of papers. "Here is some typing that I wish done."

Anger crackled between them, but she took the papers almost gratefully. While the tensions between them would never be resolved, at least she finally had something to do.

She turned toward the door, but his voice stopped her. "Where are you going?"

"I . . . I thought I'd go change clothes first."

"Why?" Amusement lightened his expression. "You look like a charming little boy—from the back."

Jennifer blushed and held the papers over her breasts, accentuated by the clinging T-shirt, and then was furious with herself for the instinctive gesture. "Where do you want me to work?"

"That desk will be fine," he said indifferently.

The last thing she wanted was to be near him all day! "Wouldn't it be better if I worked in my own room?" she offered tentatively.

"You will work here."

There was nothing for it but to do as he said. So, seething inwardly, Jennifer did as she was told. Fortunately, Kalim disappeared into the bedroom and she was left alone to puzzle out his handwriting.

The phone rang frequently, but Kalim picked it up on the extension in his room, and the many visitors were shunted in and out by Habeeb and an aide named Tajil. The atmosphere had the familiar air of a busy office and Jennifer started to relax. The work she was

123

doing had her full enthusiastic attention and at least she had a feeling of being useful. That satisfaction lasted until Ayesha arrived.

"What are you doing here?" Narrowed black eyes ranged suspiciously over Jennifer.

Jennifer stifled the many retorts that sprang to mind and said sweetly, "Why don't you ask Kalim?"

Ayesha disappeared into the bedroom and Jennifer waited for an explosion, but when none was forthcoming she resumed work. A short time later, however, she encountered a series of unfamiliar expressions. There was no way to continue without clarifying the matter so, reluctantly, she went into the bedroom.

Ayesha was curled up on the king-sized bed filing her nails and Kalim was on the phone. Hanging up the receiver, he turned to her with raised eyebrows.

"I'm . . . I'm sorry," Jennifer said, "but I've run into something that isn't quite clear."

He followed her back to the living room without comment. After she had pointed out the place, he read the copy rapidly, his hand over hers holding the papers. His explanation was succinct and she tried desperately to concentrate but the smell of his shaving lotion was like an aphrodisiac.

"Is that clear?" he asked impatiently.

Trying not to look into his eyes, her long lashes swept her cheek. "Yes, I . . . I think so."

"Well, if not, let me know." His tone was impersonal as he turned back to the bedroom—and Ayesha.

After a while they went out and Jennifer breathed a sigh of relief. Even when he was in the next room she felt Kalim's presence and was aggravated with herself for allowing him to disturb her so.

This was to set the pattern for the next two days, after which the conference was to start. Every morning Jennifer reported to his suite and he gave her office work to do. Sometimes it was dictation, but even when they worked together his attitude was as impersonal as if she were a stenographer called up from the hotel staff.

Ayesha dropped in regularly, but she treated Jennifer as part of the furnishings, ignoring her as she would a chair. Sometimes Kalim worked in the suite, but often he was gone all day. And in the evening she never saw him.

Jennifer ate dinner alone each night in the coffee shop of the hotel and then wandered disconsolately around the lobby before returning to her room. After staring in the same shop windows time after time, she almost had the displays memorized. Several men attempted to strike up an acquaintance by offering to buy her a drink but she brushed them off coolly. Even John had deserted her. She thought he had enjoyed the evening as much as she had, but evidently not because he hadn't called. At this point Jennifer would even have welcomed another visit to Charlie's American Grill as long as she didn't have to eat one more meal alone.

It was the next morning as she was preparing to go to Kalim's suite that John called. Jennifer greeted him with a warmth that surprised him as well as herself.

"You sound like you missed me," he remarked with pleasure.

"Oh, John, I did! I've been yearning to hear a friendly voice."

"Just any old friendly voice?" he teased, and before she could answer: "I was going to call you the next day but I had to fly to Abu Simbel unexpectedly and I just got back."

"Did you wind up your business?"

"No, they're still keeping me dangling," he sighed, "but at least I don't mind as much now. Will you have dinner with me tonight?"

Jennifer didn't hesitate. "I'd love to."

"That's great! A man coming back on the plane told

me about a new disco that's the in place around here. Would you like to try it?"

They made plans for the evening and when Jennifer hung up her eyes were shining like emeralds. The prospect of finally getting out of the hotel was exhilarating. Even when she entered Kalim's suite, a smile lingered on her full mouth.

Kalim was stuffing papers into a briefcase, but when he saw her one dark eyebrow rose questioningly. "You seem in a good mood for a change this morning."

Refusing to let his caustic words ruffle her, she smiled enchantingly. "I am."

"Would you like to tell me the reason?"

"You wouldn't be interested."

Shrugging indifferently, he changed the subject. "The conference starts this morning and I shall be gone all day. I will not need you so you are free to do as you please, but be here early tomorrow morning. I will wish to discuss the wording of the releases with you before the second session." She nodded and he picked up the briefcase and tucked it under his arm. But at the door he turned back. "Jennifer . . . be careful. Do not go to the native quarter and do not stay out too late."

He was laying down the law again as if she were a wayward teenager! Wasn't it bad enough that he kept her on a chain, penned up like a criminal in a plush cell? Was he afraid if he took his eyes off her she might enjoy herself? But there was no point in defying him overtly—he had all the weapons.

Gritting her teeth, Jennifer took the only barbed shot she could think of. Raising one hand in a smart salute, she said, "Yes, sir, General Kahira."

His eyes glittered and he took a step toward her. Then with a muttered imprecation, he went out and slammed the door so hard that the crystals on the chandelier tinkled.

But even Kalim's anger couldn't dampen her spirits

this morning. Faced with unexpected freedom, Jennifer decided to go shopping. Mr. Graystock had said the office would pay for some new clothes, within reason, and she had yet to buy anything. A new dress was definitely in order.

Browsing through a large department store a short time later, Jennifer was in shopper's heaven. The dresses displayed for her inspection were all so divine that she couldn't make a decision. Since the whole day belonged to her, she tried them all on and then was more confused than ever. The red chiffon was stunning and so was the black silk, but did she really want black again?

And then the saleslady brought out *the* dress. It had a tight-fitting short-sleeved white lace top with a full navy organza skirt billowing out below the hips. It fit like a dream and the only thing wrong with it was the price. Translating the numbers into American money, she gulped. By no stretch of the imagination would Mr. Graystock consider this "within reason" but Jennifer knew she had to have this dress. With remarkable logic she managed to convince herself that it was actually a bargain because the office would pay at least part of the bill. And if she went without lunches for the rest of her life, the rest of it could be written off.

Shoes were the next quest, and although it was amazing how much a few straps of silk and a couple of spike heels could cost, she bought those too.

The afternoon passed happily and when Jennifer returned to the hotel she was her usual sunny self. Kalim and his dangerous attraction was pushed to the back of her mind and all her natural optimism returned. She was going out on a date in a brand-new outfit and it was going to be fun!

When she met John in the lobby that evening, his face confirmed what her mirror had advised. Without any conceit, Jennifer knew she looked smashing.

"You're beautiful," he said. "How did I ever get so lucky?"

Jennifer smiled appreciatively. His glance held pure admiration, not the sensual appraisal she would have gotten from Kalim. Then she frowned in annoyance at herself. Why did that man always keep popping into her mind?

The nightclub was a long taxi ride from the hotel and John was sure they were being taken for a ride in more ways than one.

"Cabbies are the same all over the world," he complained, "but these guys ought to have a license to carry a gun. They're real hold-up artists. I bet he took us five miles out of our way."

"I haven't recognized anything we've passed," she soothed, "maybe it really is this far."

"I wouldn't bet on it. You just can't trust these people."

Jennifer was uncomfortable, worrying that the driver might have overheard, but fortunately they reached their destination a short time later.

The Pyramid Club, as the place was called, was already crowded. Loud disco music reverberated through the dark room and flickering strobe lights picked out each patron momentarily. There was a crowd of people in the entry and they could barely get in the door. Trust John to find an American-type disco, Jennifer thought wryly.

Inching their way slowly forward, they finally reached the front and a tuxedoed maitre d' asked, "You have a reservation, sir?"

"No, I . . . I didn't know it was necessary," John faltered.

"I am sorry, sir, but as you can see, we are full."

"But surely you can find a table somewhere," John protested. "We're Americans."

Jennifer tried to make herself as small as possible. It

wasn't John's fault, she told herself—he just didn't understand. Trying to look anywhere but at the major-domo, her glance swept the room—and then stopped in dismay. Kalim was sitting with a party of friends, observing their difficulties.

She wanted to sink into the floor, but no such easy fate awaited her. As she plucked at John's sleeve, murmuring a request to go somewhere else, Kalim appeared at their side.

"What is the problem, Abdul?"

The man spread his hands eloquently. "These people have no reservation, Mr. Kahira. I was explaining that we are full."

"There is no difficulty. They can join my table."

"No!" The words were forced explosively from Jennifer.

John looked confused until Kalim turned to him with studied charm. "Allow me to introduce myself. I am Kalim Al Kahira, Jennifer's employer. I would be most delighted if you would join my party."

A pleased acceptance colored John's voice. "Well, now, that's very friendly of you."

"But we can't accept," Jennifer added stiffly.

"Why not?" John was clearly puzzled.

"Indeed . . . why not?" Kalim echoed, but his voice was as mocking as his raised eyebrow.

"Mr. Kahira has his own party and we can't intrude," she told John meaningfully, hoping he would take the hint. "We can go somewhere else."

"But we had that long cab ride out here," he protested. "If he wants us to join him, why don't we?"

"An excellent idea." Before Jennifer could protest any further, Kalim took her elbow and steered her toward the table.

After explaining the situation to his friends, Kalim called for two more chairs and everyone moved over to accommodate them. Without quite realizing how it had happened so fast, Jennifer found herself sitting next to Kalim with John on her other side.

Kalim was making the introductions and from the impressed look on John's face, she realized that he recognized many of the names.

"Why didn't you tell me you worked for Kahira?" he whispered in her ear.

"It never came up," she muttered.

"This is really great! These contacts could be invaluable."

Jennifer hoped that Kalim hadn't heard, but from the amused look on his face, the hope was a vain one. And when he asked, in a voice pitched for her ears alone, "What is it that he wishes us to do for him?" she went warm with embarrassment.

"John is working temporarily at the Egyptian Museum," she announced to the table at large.

Polite interest followed her statement and as the other guests asked questions and John expanded visibly Kalim murmured, "It is interesting to see what kind of man attracts you. I have wondered."

"Then I'm way ahead of you," she answered bitterly. "I already know what kind of woman attracts *you.*" For the first time she realized that Ayesha wasn't by his side, and before she could stop herself she asked, "Where is your girl friend tonight?"

"If you mean Ayesha—she is otherwise engaged."

"Too bad."

"Oh, I don't know. I am bearing up under it," he said dryly.

The casual words merely added fuel to her anger. What he was telling her was that no one woman was that important to him. She had known it, of course, but hearing it put so bluntly into words made her suddenly desolate.

Her downcast eyes were on her lap when she felt

Kalim's warm hand close on her wrist. "Will you dance with me?" he asked.

The disco band had been replaced by an orchestra that was playing soft music and several couples were circling the floor.

"I . . . I don't think . . ."

But he pulled her gently to her feet. "Once before we had a truce and it was very enjoyable. Can we not have another one tonight?" Without waiting for her reply, Kalim said to John, "You do not mind if I dance with Jennifer?"

John paused in the story he was telling and said, "Oh, sure, go ahead."

Kalim led her onto the floor and she went into his arms with a remembered feeling. Her body molded itself to his and as he held her close they moved as one person. His hard muscular shoulder supported her cheek and she relaxed in his embrace, all animosity drowned in a wave of pure happiness. It's just sexual attraction, the stern voice of caution tried to warn her, but the feel of his strong fingers gently stroking her neck under the long tumbling hair blotted out the silly warning. If this was temptation, she knew why there were so many damned souls. A spreading pleasure enveloped her body at the touch of his hard thighs against hers and his warm mouth resting on her temple.

"I've missed you, little one."

She raised drugged eyes to his. "I've seen you every day."

"Not like this." His mouth slid down to her cheek.

"Kalim, you mustn't."

He brushed the pale hair away from her ear and said, "Yes, my darling, I must."

"People will see us," she murmured, only half caring.

"Why does that bother you?"

"You're the one it should bother," she said, avoiding the question. "All your friends are sitting over there."

"And each man is envious of me. You are utterly adorable."

He was doing it to her again. Making her glow with appreciation and read a meaning into his words that wasn't there. But Jennifer knew better than to fall into that trap again.

Steeling herself against his charm, she said lightly, "Is this how you get your secretaries to work harder? By paying them extravagant compliments?"

He stopped dancing right in the middle of the floor and looked at her intently. "Jennifer, why do you try to read something devious into everything I say to you?"

Her own words echoed churlishly in her ears and she felt suddenly ashamed. Unable to meet his eyes, she ducked her head and murmured, "I'm sorry."

Putting his hand under her chin, he forced her to look at him. "Do you hate me so much that you find it impossible even to be civil?"

"Oh, no!" Wide emerald eyes begged for his understanding. "I don't hate you, Kalim, I . . ." Just in time she caught herself.

"Are you afraid of me then? Is that why you are so defensive?"

"No!" Under that penetrating gaze, Jennifer couldn't lie, and she added reluctantly, "Well, maybe just a little. Sometimes you're so cold and distant. I think it would be easier if you came right out and yelled at me."

The frown disappeared from his forehead. "My poor little one, I did not realize." He drew her close, folding both arms around her. "You have aroused many emotions in me, but never coldness, I can assure you. There have been times when I wanted to put you over my knee and spank you, but yell at you? Never!"

Jennifer smiled tremulously. "I guess we have had a rather turbulent relationship."

"And perhaps we always shall have. You are like a spirited little filly, but in spite of what you think, I do not want to break your spirit."

She wrinkled her nose at him. "I don't know if I like that—being compared to a horse!"

"You complain when I pay you compliments and you complain when I do not." He laughed. "Is there no way I can please you?"

Looking into his dancing eyes, Jennifer felt her heart turn over. If he only knew how much he pleased her! Just being in his arms made her feel as though she were floating a foot above the ground and the warm male scent of him was like a love potion.

The strong emotions he awakened were mirrored in Jennifer's guileless face in spite of her desperate attempt to hide them and Kalim's laughter died as he looked at her parted lips. He drew a sharp breath, and then, putting his hand on her flushed cheek, he stroked it with gentle fingers.

"There is magic between us that cannot be denied," he said.

Jennifer was drowning in his magnetism, but she made a desperate attempt to save herself. "Magic is just a form of deception," she told him, wondering which one of them she was trying to convince.

The smile he gave her was indulgent. "And you do not like deceptions?"

"No, I don't." Her answer was automatic, but his next words punctured her smug assurance.

"And yet you are willing to deceive yourself," he said softly.

The man was a devil! Could he see into her very soul? Jennifer's eyes fell before his penetrating gaze. "I . . . I don't know what you're talking about."

He shook his head pityingly. "Jennifer, Jennifer, you are like a little child standing at the top of a slide—afraid to try it, yet reluctant to climb back down."

"I'm not a child and life is not a playground." Her chin set stubbornly.

"It could be." His hands moved compellingly over her tense back. "I could open up a new world for you if you would let me."

Jennifer had already caught a glimpse of heaven in his seductive arms. She shivered, remembering those provocative caresses on her eager body and the feel of his warm mouth trailing kisses that aroused her almost unbearably. Yes, it would be heaven—at first. And then it would be hell! Because Jennifer realized sadly that she loved him with every ounce of her being while he felt only a passing desire. Once that was satisfied, she would be just another woman to be enjoyed and cast aside for the next conquest. And Jennifer knew she would surely die if that happened. No, it was better never to know the full ecstasy. Unconsciously, she shook her head.

He was watching her intently. "The answer is no? Well, so be it, but at least from now on we can be friends."

"I . . . I'd like that." The smile she gave him was uncertain but his was genuine.

"We will enjoy each other's company and I will endeavor to forget that you have the face of an angel and the body of Circe."

"Please, Kalim!" The strangled words were scarcely audible.

Kissing her lightly on the tip of her nose, he laughed. "Very well, my shy little darling, I shall embarrass you no longer."

Kalim was as good as his word. For the rest of the evening he put himself out to be charming. He was the ultimate host—witty, amusing, and solicitous. John was dazzled, and even Jennifer, knowing this was all a game to Kalim, couldn't help falling deeper under his spell.

The evening passed much too swiftly and Jennifer

savored every moment of it, liberated from the tensions that usually beset her when she was in Kalim's company. Conversation flowed freely around the table and when Kalim rested his arm on the back of her chair or put his hand lightly over hers, it was purely a casual, nonthreatening gesture. Yet perversely she yearned for more.

What on earth is wrong with me, Jennifer wondered impatiently. This is what I wanted, isn't it—for us to be friends and nothing more? But the nearness of that powerful male body made her pulses race without any effort at all on his part.

I'll get over it, she vowed staunchly, but looking up, she caught a sardonic look on his darkly handsome face. Or was she just imagining it? Kalim was now returning her glance with open camaraderie.

When the evening was over they discovered that Kalim had picked up the check for the entire party. John made a token protest, which Kalim graciously overrode, and the farewells were polite and general.

"What a great guy that Kahira is," John exclaimed on the way home. "You're really lucky to be working for him."

She murmured something noncommittal and he continued to sing Kalim's praises all the way to the hotel. Jennifer's lips curved upward in the covering darkness. It had been a wonderful evening.

Chapter Eight

Jennifer awoke with a smile on her face. Stretching contentedly, she tried to remember the dream responsible for this pleasurable feeling. Suddenly her eyelids flew open. It was no dream! Last night had marked a turning point in her relationship with Kalim.

All the coldness and cruelty were gone and instead he had treated her with kindness and affection. The word gave her pause, reminding her of her own stronger feelings toward him. Well, it was better than nothing.

Raising her legs and clasping her arms around them, Jennifer rested her cheek on one knee. Time was running out and soon all she would have left were memories. But at least these last ones would be glorious, unmarred by the savage exchanges that had tormented her in the beginning. And when it came time to leave . . . The rosy glow faded. How could she even contemplate a life without him?

Her whole being rebelled against the thought, but Jennifer forced her mind to accept the fact and plan ahead. When Kalim sent her away she would have to find the strength to manage a graceful good-bye—that much she owed to both of them. He must never know that an integral part of her was dying. With a shuddering sigh she reached for her slippers.

Under the stinging shower spray her spirits lifted. There was at least a week left, perhaps more—a week of seeing him every day, hearing his voice and inhaling the heady male scent of him. A little thrill started down her back and a smile lifted the corners of her mouth.

Selecting a cool sleeveless pink dress, Jennifer dressed quickly. She spared a few moments to brush her hair until it shone like a pale satin ribbon and then hurried to Kalim's rooms.

Her timid knock was answered by a brusque voice telling her to enter. Kalim was seated at the desk going over some reports and he glanced up, scowling impatiently at the interruption. But when he saw Jennifer, he stood and greeted her. Capturing both of her hands, he looked her over so appreciatively that her cheeks soon matched the dress.

"You are up early."

"You told me you wanted to go over the releases this morning," she explained, the warm glow spreading down her ivory throat.

"So I did," he murmured, sliding his hands slowly up her arms. "Did you have a good time last night?"

"I had a wonderful time," she said simply, not bothering to play any silly games.

His mobile mouth tilted at the corners. "Because of John . . . or was it something else?"

Jennifer's long lashes fell. If he ever looked into her eyes he would know the truth instantly and that must never happen. But Kalim was not to be denied.

Putting his finger under her chin, he tried to make her look at him. "Can I hope that I contributed to your enjoyment?"

Steadying herself with a great effort, she managed to

meet his eyes but she evaded the question. "It was very kind of you to ask us to join your party. John didn't know reservations were required."

"Ah, yes, the praiseworthy John." His hands abruptly released her and he crammed them in his pockets. "You enjoy his company?"

"We have a lot in common," she said defensively.

"And you and I do not?"

"I didn't say that. It's just that . . . well, John and I speak the same language." The reasoning sounded lame even to her.

"When we danced, I thought you and I were communicating very well—even without words."

His low, sensuous voice lit a slow fire in her veins and Jennifer tried not to remember the rapture that had enveloped her when he held her close. The leisurely caress of those long fingers down her neck and shoulders was like a trail of kisses and her glowing skin had leaped to joyous life under their touch.

"I . . ." She paused and cleared her throat. "I was very happy that we weren't arguing, Kalim. Our brief acquaintance is almost over, but I'd like to think that we parted friends."

His hands cupped her face and his eyes bored into hers, seemingly to the depths of her soul. "Is that all you want from me, Jennifer—friendship?"

She gave him a wan smile. "Is it too much to ask?"

His thumbs massaged her cheeks gently. "You try my patience, you disturb my sleep, you interfere with my work, and you want us to be *friends?*"

His tantalizing touch made her breathing quicken and she gave a shaky laugh. "That's what friends are for. Just think if we were enemies."

A long forefinger traced the shape of her mouth, pulling her lower lip down gently until her mouth parted at his touch. "That we will never be, my love."

His arm circled her waist, drawing her closer to the hard column of his body and Jennifer started to tremble. She knew she ought to resist but it was futile. Every inch of her longed for him. Was it too much to ask for just one more touch? His hand tangled in her silken hair, supporting her as his mouth took hard possession of hers, demanding a response that she was only too happy to give. His other hand caressed her slender waist, then moved up to stroke the swelling curve of her breast. A shock of desire ran through her and she strained closer, needing to store up the memories that had to last a lifetime.

Thrusting her fingers through his thick hair, she uttered incoherent little moans and his passion increased to meet her own. Running his mouth down her smooth throat, he kissed the throbbing pulse that beat just for him. His warm lips slid down to the hollow between her breasts and she cried out with pleasure and twined her arms around his neck.

But as she trembled in anticipation, Kalim suddenly put her away from him and drew a shuddering, ragged breath. "Jennifer, Jennifer, my little innocent, you do not know what you are doing." She looked at him blindly. How could he stop now when she wanted him so? Shaking his head, he drew her gently into his arms and stroked her hair. "Not this way, my darling, not this way."

She leaned against him helplessly, waiting for her thundering heart to return to normal. Fully expecting a wave of guilt to follow, Jennifer was surprised when it didn't. She had given herself in complete surrender and he had refused the gift. Why didn't she feel that crushing sense of shame? Was it because she had suddenly grown up and realized the feelings that could grip a man and a woman?

Kalim knew, of course, but he hadn't used it to his

advantage. Neither of them was to blame for this wave of passion that had rolled over them, but recognizing her inexperience, he hadn't taken what was his for the asking. How much she had to learn about this man!

She looked up at him wonderingly as he gently tucked a vagrant strand of hair behind her ear. "I must leave you now. Unfortunately, I have to go to work."

"The releases!" Jennifer cried. "We didn't go over the releases."

His smile was gently mocking. "I wonder how it slipped our minds?" She blushed and he planted a light kiss on her cheek. "No matter—we will do it when I return this afternoon. Will you wait for me?"

Her eyes met his and she smiled. "I'll be here."

After Kalim left, Jennifer was too keyed up to begin work immediately. Her body still tingled from his touch and her mouth enjoyed the aftertaste of his kisses. Standing motionless, she wondered what complete possession would be like? A quiver in the pit of her stomach warned her that it was too compelling to dwell on.

Deciding that she would be better off working than thinking, Jennifer approached the desk. Kalim had given her a very complicated statistical chart to type and now seemed the perfect time. She needed something that would demand her full concentration. While putting the scattered pages in order, she discovered that one was missing. Perhaps Kalim had taken it into the other room to make some notations.

Jennifer started for his bedroom in a very business-like manner and then stopped on the threshold. The maid hadn't been in to clean yet and return it to the sterile impersonality that is the goal of every hotel throughout the world, so the room was still imbued with his presence.

His pajama bottoms were cast carelessly over a chair,

although no top was in evidence. For a moment Jennifer had a vision of that bare bronzed chest, but she shook her head to dispel it. The bed was rumpled and the pillow still bore the imprint of his head. It drew her like a magnet.

As she was reaching out to touch it, unable to stop herself, an imperious voice rang out. "What are you doing in here?" Ayesha demanded.

Snatching her hand back, Jennifer said, "I . . . I was looking for a missing page of a report."

"Did you expect to find it in the bed?" The question was contemptuous, as though the other girl recognized her need for any contact with him. Without waiting for a reply, she asked curtly, "Where is Kalim?"

"He went to the conference."

"Those stupid meetings," the dark-haired girl muttered under her breath. Then, with a mercurial change of subject: "When are you going home?"

Jennifer clenched her hands but managed to answer calmly, "I don't know. Why don't you ask Mr. Kahira?"

"I wouldn't bother him with anything so trivial."

Jennifer shrugged and turned toward the door, too angry to trust herself to reply. But Ayesha stopped her. "Just how well do you know Kalim?"

"Not very," Jennifer admitted, remembering all his complexities.

"I thought so." A smug smile crossed the other girl's face. "It did not help you to run after him, did it?"

"Just exactly what are you implying?"

"Kalim is a very handsome man," Ayesha said. "I have always known that he is irresistible to women, but he cannot be blamed if silly girls take his attentions seriously."

"Meaning me?" Jennifer's eyes glittered like emeralds under a neon light.

"You would know that better than I." Ayesha's air of confidence was enamel hard. "I was only trying to do a good deed by warning you." If so, it was probably the first good deed she had ever done, Jennifer thought cynically, but Ayesha's added words were chilling. "Kalim belongs to me. Our families look favorably on our union and I am the one he will marry."

"And it doesn't bother you that he makes love to . . . other women?"

The barb hit home and Jennifer was delighted to see her rival's face turn scarlet. "Then it is true! You *have* been allowing him into your bed."

"What a quaint expression," Jennifer said coolly, although inside she was bubbling with glee.

"You are a fool if you think you can take him from me," Ayesha hissed.

"Are you so sure of that?"

They were both flushed and anger crackled between them like lightning. "He is merely playing with you as he has played with all the others. *I* am the one he will return to, you will see!" Ayesha shouted before sweeping out the door.

Jennifer was trembling after the ugly scene and she took a deep breath to steady herself. What the other girl had said was probably true, she realized, to her sorrow. It had been childish to pretend that she and Kalim were having an affair, but Jennifer didn't regret it. Ayesha had everything—including Kalim—but even that didn't satisfy her. She was spoiled and rude and deserved to be put down. But it didn't change anything.

Ayesha had subtly poisoned the atmosphere, and when Jennifer wandered over to the typewriter a little later, she couldn't seem to get started. Thoughts of Kalim kept crowding out everything else, but they were no longer joyous ones. She kept remembering the way he had touched her and kissed her, but the memories were tinged now with melancholy. Was she really just a light flirtation to him? Wasn't there anything more than sex involved?

When Kalim returned in the late afternoon, Jennifer was hard at work, trying to make up for the wasted morning. Habeeb accompanied him as always, but after checking the room with a sweeping glance, he quietly disappeared.

"You should not still be working, little one," Kalim chided her.

"You said I was to wait for you."

"Yes, but I did not expect you to slave the full time." His eyes teased her gently. "I thought you would be eating bonbons and reading French novels."

"I don't read French that well and bonbons are fattening," she laughed back at him.

His seducing hands were at her waist and his eyes were aglow as he said, "That is one thing you do not have to worry about."

But Jennifer stepped back. Ayesha's spiteful words were too fresh in her memory, although every instinct pleaded for a repeat of this morning's rapture. "Hadn't we better go over the releases?"

One eyebrow rose and he rubbed the knuckle of a forefinger along the line of her jaw. "Are you sure that is what you want to do?"

Jennifer forced her voice to remain even. "If we don't get to it, we're going to be way behind. Besides, I really want to know what's going on."

Reluctantly, he held out a chair for her and, seating himself at her side, took some papers out of his briefcase. "You are right, my sweet."

The next hour was stimulating. Kalim explained what had gone on at the conference and Jennifer was fascinated by this glimpse into international relations. It was exciting to be in on matters of such urgency. Personal feelings were put aside for the moment as they worked together.

"Are you telling me that it is insulting to say, 'We must exact a fair share against each country?' " His piercing eyes examined her face.

"I didn't say insulting, Kalim, but *exact* isn't the best word you could use. In English it means to demand. And I don't think I would say '*against* each country.' That makes for adversaries and you want allies. Wouldn't it be better to say, 'We are requesting that each nation contribute its fair share'? Some of them won't—we know that—but at least you aren't giving them any excuse to get huffy."

Kalim looked at her with approval and planted a congratulatory kiss on her forehead. "Jennifer, you are a genius! I am going to raise your salary."

"That won't be necessary," she said, pleased by his reaction. "It's about time I started earning it."

When they finally finished work, Kalim leaned back in satisfaction. "This has been very enlightening. You have earned a good dinner. Will you have it with me, Jennifer?"

She wanted it more than anything in the world, but not this way. "You don't have to reward me. I was only doing my job."

He took her hand and kissed the palm, then clasped it between both of his. "If I ever want to reward you, it will be with more than dinner."

In a low husky tone she said, "I just meant . . . you mustn't feel you have to . . ."

As her voice trailed off, he lifted her to her feet, saying, "It is always a struggle to get you to accept anything. I know this from experience. Therefore I am *ordering* you to wear your prettiest dress and be ready to dine with me at nine o'clock."

A wave of happiness suffused her and she looked at him with a smile. "Well, since you put it that way, I have no choice, do I?"

"None whatever," he assured her.

Jennifer was ready long before the appointed hour, nervousness turning her hands to ice. This would be the first time she had been alone with Kalim since he had taken her sight-seeing. Of course, they were alone at times in his suite, but that was more like being in an office with people going in and out and the telephone providing a constant intrusion. This was different. Tonight would be like a real date.

Kalim called for her promptly and waited politely at the door while she gathered her things. He wore a dark suit, unlike the casual clothes she was used to seeing on him in the suite. The rich fabric accentuated his broad shoulders and the narrow trousers were molded to his powerful thigh muscles, making his masculinity almost overpowering. Jennifer felt suddenly shy and, as if he were aware of it, Kalim kept up a steady flow of conversation to put her at ease.

Leading her across the lobby, he chatted about inconsequential things and Jennifer's tension gradually lessened. They were almost to the door when René dashed up to them.

"Kalim, don't tell me I have finally found you!"

"What is wrong, René?"

"Not a thing now," the Frenchman said cheerfully. "It is just that I have been looking for you all day and leaving messages with that *sauvage*, Habeeb. Doesn't he ever give them to you?"

Kalim smothered a smile. "Sometimes, when he knows I am busy and he considers it unimportant, Habeeb hesitates to disturb me."

"Well, I like that!" René exclaimed. "It would serve you right if we had gone without you this evening." When Kalim looked blank, his friend rolled his eyes toward heaven in a Gallic gesture of annoyance. "I suppose you have forgotten that we go to The Eye of Osiris tonight?"

Kalim's embarrassed glance at Jennifer clearly indicated that he had indeed forgotten and her heart plummeted. He had made a previous date for tonight, but it wasn't really his fault. He had much on his mind these days and she must make it as easy as possible. "It's all right. I don't mind, Kalim, truly I don't."

But his hand closed around her wrist as she would have turned away. "Where do you think you are going? It is true that I had forgotten these plans, but it changes nothing."

"But if you already have a date for tonight," she protested.

Kalim's eyes smiled into hers and his tone was one of finality. "You are my date."

"Splendid!" René seized both of her hands with typical impetuosity. "The little golden doll will, how you say—dress up the act! And if Kalim is not good to you, I shall steal you away from him."

The two men led her up to the waiting group and Jennifer's delight at being included died a swift death when she saw that Ayesha was part of it. The perfect evening started to crumble until she noticed that the other girl was standing next to a tall blond man who had his hand on her arm. He was introduced as Hans Von Slagen.

Amidst general confusion, the party all separated into various cars and then reassembled after a short drive. The Eye of Osiris was a nightclub and Jennifer found out that the big attraction was a beautiful belly dancer who was currently the toast of Cairo.

They were shown to a large table and as usual Ayesha maneuvered it so that she was sitting beside Kalim, but Jennifer refused to let it bother her. It promised to be an exciting evening and she was determined not to let the spiteful brunette spoil it for her.

Conversation around the table was general and to her surprise Jennifer didn't feel ill at ease. Everyone seemed genuinely interested in her. René asked questions about San Francisco since it had been a long time since he had been there, and his companion, a petite redhead named Martine, added her own queries.

"Do you still have those charming shops in Chinatown?" René asked. "So amazing," he told the others. "The amount of beautiful things is unbelievable."

"Kalim can give you a report on that. I gave him the deluxe tour." Jennifer's eyes met Kalim's and they smiled at the shared memory.

His hand covered hers where it was lying on the table, but before he could answer Ayesha plucked at his sleeve. "You haven't said yet if you are going to join us on the Riviera next month."

Jennifer attempted to retrieve her hand, but his tightened over it as she was forced to answer René's questions herself. They talked about Chinatown and other places she had taken Kalim and Martine said, "Has he shown you Cairo? He owes it to you after all your kind hospitality."

"He took me to see the Pyramids and to lunch at a wonderful restaurant, the . . ." Jennifer's soft brow furrowed and she looked to Kalim to supply the name.

Once again Ayesha interrupted. "Kalim, my love, you simply must settle an argument for us."

But he surveyed her with a glint in his eye that displayed his impatience. "Ayesha, may I remind you that Hans is your escort this evening? I suggest that you talk to him." When she turned an ugly red, his tone softened slightly, but the steel in it was still evident. "When you were a child I taught you many things. How did I overlook manners?"

Ayesha was breathing hard, but she chose to take his words as a joke. Glancing at Jennifer, who was trying to hide her embarrassment, a sly look came into the snapping black eyes. "It is true, Kalim taught me everything I know." The gaze she gave him through her thick lashes was sensually provocative as she added, "And if I can please him, I can please any man."

The laughter was general and Jennifer forced herself to join in, although she felt faintly sick. Was it true? Were she and Kalim lovers? Had he held her and touched her in the same way that he had caressed Jennifer? A lump rose in her throat and she looked down at the hands clasped in her lap.

Kalim's arm was around her shoulders and his mouth close to her ear. "I am sorry," he said softly.

Sorry that Ayesha had been rude to her? Sorry that he had made a small scene and knew Jennifer was embarrassed by it? Or sorry because she knew he and Ayesha were lovers? She raised troubled eyes to his but could find no answer.

They had proceeded through many courses of exotic food and the waiter was removing the last of the dishes when a loud drumroll announced the start of the floor show. Expectant faces were turned to the dance floor and the pulsing music took on an excited beat.

The curtains parted and a beautiful raven-haired girl made her sinuous way to the middle of the floor. A spotlight caught the bejeweled gold belt that sat low on her rounded hips. Long gauzy scarves were attached to the belt and they swirled around her bare legs as her body twisted sensuously. A low-cut bra matched the belt and her full breasts strained against their confinement as she undulated to the throbbing music.

It was a seductive dance and the beautiful, lithe body, so liquidly supple, made its invitation unmistakable. The exotic girl twirled around the outer edge of the floor, pausing to trail her scarves tantalizingly over some of the men at the ringside tables, but when she reached Kalim, he was the recipient of her full efforts. Swaying invitingly, she performed as though for his eyes alone. He smiled indulgently and Jennifer admired his aplomb since he was the center of attention.

When the show was over, they all agreed that the performer deserved her acclaim.

"It might look easy, but it isn't," Martine declared. "I took lessons once and I was sore for a week."

"What marvelous exercise though. All that twisting and turning should really flatten the tummy," Jennifer remarked.

The men's comments were predictably different and everyone laughed. Jennifer enjoyed every moment of the evening and wondered how she could ever have felt strange with these people.

When it was time to leave, she looked at Kalim with shining eyes. "Thank you for a marvelous evening."

His mouth tilted upward in amusement. "You are supposed to say that when I take you home."

"I couldn't wait," she said simply. "I know this is just another evening to you, but it's been a real treat for me. Everyone's been so nice to me."

"You make it very easy." He took her hands and there was such warmth in his gaze that Jennifer felt her pulses quicken. "But you are wrong about one thing." She looked at him questioningly. "It was not just another evening for me."

Happiness settled around her like a velvet cloak, but she was gripped with shyness. Sensing her sudden confusion, Kalim put his arm lightly around her shoulders and led her from the restaurant.

The entire party went back to the hotel for a nightcap in the bar, but after a very short time Kalim made their excuses, pleading an early-morning appointment. The others stayed on and Ayesha watched their departure with calculating eyes.

As they got off the elevator Jennifer felt her breath catch in her throat. For the first time all night she and

Kalim were truly alone—but it was only for a moment, common sense reminded her. The evening was over. Was he planning on kissing her good night? Jennifer was appalled at the fierce hunger that swept her at the thought and knew it must be avoided at all costs. If he touched her, if that warm mouth covered her own, parting her lips in that experienced way he had of arousing desires that demanded fulfillment . . . She put the image determinedly out of her mind.

They had reached Kalim's door and Jennifer stopped when he would have gone on. Turning to him, she extended her hand. "Good night, Kalim, and thank you again."

Raising one eyebrow sardonically, he said, "I know that women's liberation is very big in your country, but in mine a gentleman walks a lady to her door, not vice versa."

"But I'm just down the hall."

"Nevertheless." Taking her arm firmly, he walked her to her room and held out his hand. "The key."

She produced it reluctantly and as their fingers touched she pulled her hand away quickly and then was furious with herself. He looked at her in amused awareness and her cheeks flushed a delicate pink. Ducking her head, Jennifer tried to hide her embarrassment from him, but it was no use.

Kalim broke the small silence and his voice was wry. "You are a small enchantress, Jennifer. One moment you are a beautiful, provocative woman, the next, a bashful little child. Which one is the real you?"

"I don't know." Her voice was strangled.

"I think you do, but you are afraid to admit the truth even to yourself." His voice was low and sensual. "You were made for love. Why are you so frightened of it?" She half turned in flight, but his firm hands on her shoulders prevented it. "No, no, do not run away from me."

"It's late," she whispered.

Ignoring her protest, his dark eyes swept her body and every nerve quickened as though he had actually touched her. "You have beautiful breasts," he remarked almost absently. "They were made to be caressed." Her breath caught as she remembered that he knew exactly what she looked like. His hands slid up her slender neck and, cupping her face in his palms, he inspected it thoughtfully. "You have the face of a golden-haired angel. What man could resist that lovely mouth?"

His dark head moved down and Jennifer panicked. "No . . . no, you mustn't."

His fathomless black eyes smiled compellingly into hers. "Why do you deny yourself the pleasure you want—and I can give you?"

"I don't . . . you can't!" The words tumbled out wildly. Jennifer knew that if he kissed her she would be lost. Once he took her in his arms, she would surrender completely, allowing the fire in her blood to engulf her. Even now her fingers ached to grasp that thick dark hair and draw his head down to hers.

But Kalim released her. A faint smile played over his firm mouth as he regarded her with enigmatic eyes. "Do not struggle so desperately, little dove. I will free you—this time."

A long forefinger caressed the curve of her cheek and he leaned down and kissed her gently. Then he was gone.

Jennifer's heart pounded and she was filled with a mixture of regret and relief. This was what she wanted —of course it was! But her treacherous body denied it, filled as it was with a mindless yearning for his touch. It took all her willpower not to run after him, but he never looked back.

Chapter Nine

When she reported for work the next day, Jennifer wasn't sure what to expect. Kalim was a master at keeping her off balance. Whenever she thought their relationship had stabilized, he threw her another curve.

He was on the phone and he greeted her with a friendly smile and a wave toward the coffeepot sitting on the room-service table. Jennifer poured herself a cup. When Kalim got off the telephone, he began to discuss the conference.

There was no hint of last night in his manner. He was pleasant but impersonal. An outsider would never have imagined that they knew each other more than casually —and would certainly not have believed the suggestive words he had used to describe her. Jennifer was almost convinced that she had dreamed the whole thing.

The conference was in recess for a day, so Kalim worked in the suite and Jennifer was kept busy. Phones rang constantly and visitors shuttled in and out. It was almost like politics at election time, she thought. Sometimes a collection of representatives from various countries would be meeting in one room while a second group would be conferring in another. In spite of the exotic locale, it was a familiar situation and very heady stuff to be on the inside of such important proceedings.

She and Kalim met rarely, with only time to smile in passing, but Jennifer had the impression that they were functioning as a team, and she had a warm feeling from his approving glance that he felt the same way. The only jarring note was Ayesha, who drifted in and made a nuisance of herself, but Kalim got rid of her somehow when Jennifer's back was turned.

At the end of the long day, when they finally found themselves alone, Kalim complimented her. "You did very well. You were of great assistance to me."

"I'm glad. I really enjoyed it," she said sincerely.

With arms crossed behind his head, he leaned back against the couch and stretched his long legs out, regarding her reflectively. "All that beauty and brains too—I cannot believe it."

"A typically chauvinist remark." Her eyes sparkled with green fire.

"Ah, yes, I had forgotten. You are a women's liberationist. You do not wish to be one of the dancing girls in my harem."

Suddenly raging curiosity got the better of her. "Do you really have a harem, Kalim?"

White teeth blazed in his tan face as he laughed at her. "In this day and age, what man could afford one?" he teased. "There are still some countries where four wives are permitted, but that is a pale imitation of the harems of old."

Jennifer gasped. "That's just as bad! That's . . . it's bigamy! Why would a woman put up with that?"

Stretching out his arms, he said lazily, "Come here and I will show you."

"I don't think that's very funny," she said stiffly.

He threw back his head and laughed out loud. "I was only answering your question."

"No, you weren't. I'm serious and you're not. I can't think of anything sadder than being in love with a man and having to share him with three other women."

He uncoiled his long frame and got up from the couch. "I only said the law *allowed* four wives. I did not say that every man took advantage of it."

"That doesn't matter," she told him earnestly. "It would always be hanging over her head, the fact that he might."

"I do not think you would have to worry, Jennifer." He smoothed her long hair, curling a shining strand around his fingers. "If a man were married to you, it would be the other wives who would have the complaint. You would keep him busy every night."

As angry as she was at him, his intimate touch set off a thunder in her veins and she was drowning in the compelling look he gave her. Fortunately the phone rang and the magnetic contact was broken. Jennifer moved away from him as he picked up the receiver.

After listening for a moment, his annoyed expression changed to one of pleasure. "I was waiting for your call," he said. "I am looking forward to seeing you."

His voice was warm and directions followed for a meeting place. Jennifer turned away and busied herself at the desk to give Kalim a measure of privacy. He was obviously making dinner plans and she didn't want to intrude. At least it wasn't with Ayesha. Jennifer would have known from that special tolerant quality his voice took on when he talked to the clinging brunette. Was it some other woman though? Jennifer realized with a sinking heart that she did indeed share something with Ayesha—jealousy!

A sharp pain gripped her as he said, "I am sorry that I cannot take you to dinner tonight, Jennifer. Someone I have been wanting very much to talk to is—"

But she interrupted, unwilling to hear the details. Turning away, she managed an air of indifference.

"Don't give it another thought." And before he could respond, she was out the door.

This pattern held for the next week. The days were busy and fruitful but the nights were always filled with suspense. She never knew ahead of time what they would hold. Sometimes Kalim invited her to dinner and they dined at the hotel or at interesting places he selected. Sometimes they were joined by his friends, at other times they dined alone. But Kalim never made a date in advance.

John called regularly to ask her out, but although she hated herself for being so weak, Jennifer would never make a commitment until the last minute. She pleaded the demands of her job and it convinced him, but she couldn't fool herself. The real reason was that she wanted to be available whenever Kalim wanted to see her. There was so little time left.

But John accepted her excuses and was willing to see her whenever she was free. On the occasions when they did go out together, Jennifer always hoped they might run across Kalim again and perhaps he would be jealous. It was a vain hope because they never did.

The conference was drawing to a close. There were only two days left and Jennifer was feeling particularly low when Kalim mentioned he had an engagement because she knew that this evening it was with Ayesha. The other girl had made a point of coming to the suite and waiting until Jennifer was within earshot to mention their plans for that night.

"Mother and Father are expecting us at eight thirty," Ayesha said, her hand on Kalim's sleeve in a possessive manner. "Try not to be late. They think you are perfect, so do not disillusion them now."

His mocking gaze slanted across her pouting face. "If they actually do think I am perfect, it is only because they had to settle for a house full of troublesome little girls. I am the son they never had."

"That can be rectified," she said smugly, kissing him lingeringly on the mouth.

Kalim laughed and swatted her playfully on the bottom. "Any man who took you on would have to have his head examined."

Jennifer kept her head carefully bent over the typewriter, pretending not to hear their bantering words, but each one hammered a splinter of pain into her heart.

Tearing the copy out of the machine, she put it in front of him, saying, "I think that about does it. I'll be leaving now."

Kalim's only comment was a pleasant good night and Jennifer averted her head, but not before she saw the triumphant look on Ayesha's face.

The phone was ringing as Jennifer opened her door and it was John, asking if she were free that evening. The prospect of spending it alone with her vivid imagination had been horrendous, so her acceptance of his invitation was especially warm. They arranged a time and when she hung up Jennifer's spirits were slightly lifted.

The evening was pleasantly uneventful as all of the ones she spent with John were, but that was part of his attraction. There was no physical magnetism, no sexual sparring. The fact that he could feel differently if she gave him half a chance made Jennifer slightly guilty, but she salved her conscience by assuring herself that she really hadn't done anything to lead him on.

John was her refuge from dangerous currents and as long as she directed the conversation toward ancient Egypt and his work, he was an interesting companion. It was only when the talk drifted toward modern times that she realized how provincial and, yes, downright narrow-minded, he was. But that was a topic she continually steered away from.

Every now and then she was unsuccessful, and as he

walked her to her door at the end of the evening, he was complaining about the Cairo weather.

"I'll admit we have rain in New Orleans, but at least you appreciate the sunshine when you see it. The sun never quits here!"

Jennifer had to agree. "It wakes me up early every morning. My drapes don't quite close and I can't make the maid understand. The aggravating thing is that I could fix it myself—the leader hook is just off the trolley, but these ceilings are at least ten feet tall and I can't reach it even when I stand on the table."

"Why didn't you mention it before? I'd be happy to fix it for you."

"Oh, John, would you? I'd really appreciate that."

"Glad to do it." He gave her a fond look. "It will give me a chance to show you what a handy man I am to have around."

Feeling slightly uncomfortable over his remark, Jennifer led him into the room. John moved the table over to stand on and, as she had said, it took only a moment to fasten the drapery hook back in the proper slot.

"There, now you can sleep till noon," he said, dragging the table back in place.

"Well, not really," she laughed, "but at least I won't be up before even a self-respecting bird is stirring. You really *are* a handy man to have around."

"I've been wanting to tell you that." He took her hands and his expression altered.

For some time John had been attempting to put their relationship on a more personal footing and Jennifer had always been able to avoid it. Now she managed to do it again.

Pinning a bright smile on her face, she pulled one hand away and used the other to guide him gently toward the door. "It's getting late and we both have to get up in the morning, although thanks to you, not quite as early."

With a sigh, he accepted his dismissal. "When am I going to see you again?"

"I don't know for certain. Why don't you call me? And John, thanks again."

Turning the knob, he stepped into the hall, his mouth twisting wryly. "Sure, glad to be of service. Just call me whenever you need someone to do a man's work."

From inside the room her laughter drifted out into the corridor. "John, you're wonderful! What would I do without you?"

"Just remember that I was here tonight when you needed me," he said jokingly.

Their words floated down the hall and belatedly Jennifer realized that it was late and they might be disturbing other people. Sticking her head around the door, she said, "Shh, someone might hear us."

Neither of them saw Kalim and Ayesha, who had gotten off the elevator as John left Jennifer's room. It was only when he turned from her with a smile and walked toward them that John noticed the other couple.

"Well, hello, it's nice to see you again," he said.

Ayesha eyed him speculatively and murmured a greeting, but Kalim's response bordered on rudeness as he inclined his head curtly, his face stormy. John was puzzled at the reception, but after a moment's hesitation, he continued on and Kalim led Ayesha to her door.

"He is quite good-looking, isn't he?" she asked with a sidelong look at Kalim. When he didn't answer, she said slyly, "At least your little secretary thinks so. I wonder what . . . service he performed for her tonight, don't you?"

Kalim's eyes glistened ominously, but he didn't rise to the bait. "Good night, Ayesha." His tone closed the subject.

Heeding the implicit warning in his voice, she

switched tactics. "Come in for a drink, chérie," she coaxed. "I am not a bit tired."

"But I am. It has been a long day."

"Surely you can spare the time for one little drink. We have not had a moment alone all night."

He looked at her with preoccupation and then leaned forward and brushed her cheek with his lips. "Good night, Ayesha. Go to bed."

As soon as John had left, Jennifer started to prepare for bed. Taking off her dress, she put the light cotton robe over her bra and panties and kicked off her high heels with a satisfied sigh. Before going into the bathroom to wash her face, she wandered over to inspect the draperies. Yes, they overlapped perfectly. John had done a good job. It was while she was inspecting his handwork that an authoritative knock sounded at the door. Who on earth could that be at this hour? She went quickly to answer it.

"Yes?" Her puzzled frown increased as Kalim pushed his way into the room and slammed the door behind him. "What . . . what are you doing here?" she faltered.

"I knew you had not gone to bed yet—or should I say to sleep?"

There was a white line around his grim mouth and it was obvious that he was keeping himself under tight rein. Without knowing the reason, fear crept through her and Jennifer's heart started to pound.

"N . . . no, I wasn't asleep."

Her hair was tousled where she had pulled her sweater over it a few minutes earlier and she automatically tried to smooth it back in place. The gesture caught his eye and he surveyed her contemptuously.

"It must have been quite a night."

She looked at him in bewilderment. "I don't understand."

His eyes blazed and under the deep tan his face was

pale. "I will admit you had me fooled and that is quite an accomplishment." The words contained pent-up rage.

"What are you talking about?"

"That frightened little virgin act," he sneered. "It was quite convincing."

"What are you saying?" she cried.

His mouth turned down derisively and he gripped her elbows, drawing her toward his hard, lean body. "John was smarter than I, wasn't he? He knew what you wanted and he gave it to you."

His fingers were biting into her soft skin and she was genuinely alarmed by the look of primitive passion staring out at her. "I have no idea what you're talking about and I don't want to know. You must have had too much to drink. I'd like you to leave."

"And if I refuse?" The sneering words were menacing and Jennifer felt the beginning of panic.

"Kalim, please, you aren't yourself—can't you see that? Please . . . don't do anything you'll regret."

He laughed out loud, but it was a bitter laugh without mirth. "The only thing I regret is all the time I have wasted. All the times you could have been warming my bed instead of disturbing my sleep." One arm went around her waist, drawing her roughly to him, and his hand fastened on her breast.

There was no love, no tenderness, just raw desire and Jennifer pounded on his chest with clenched fists. "Let go of me! What do you think you're doing?"

His arms were like steel bands and mocking eyes raked her. "Is it too soon? Did John satisfy your needs? But surely the novelty of a second man will arouse you anew."

"You must be crazy!" She was truly frightened by the madness in his eyes.

"Not any longer. I will admit I was under your spell, but now I intend to have what the others have gotten. I will lose myself in your beautiful body as I have wanted to do since we first met."

His mouth touched the wildly beating pulse at the base of her throat and slid across to her shoulders, pushing aside the thin fabric of her robe. After ruthlessly tearing open the front-fastened wispy bra, his lips found her bare breast and a shock passed through Jennifer at the warm possession of his mouth.

With a desperate effort, she twisted away from him. "Kalim!" It was like a cry of pain. "Why are you doing this to me?"

His eyes were hard and scornful as he answered her question with one of his own. "Why are you continuing this pretense? Do you think I am a complete fool? I will admit I have acted like one, but that is all over now."

Jennifer pulled at her robe and strained against his hard embrace. "I don't know what's happened to you."

"Don't you?" His mouth turned down in a bitter smile. "I have merely come to my senses, and although I admit to being sadly disillusioned, I shall endeavor to put it out of my mind as I enjoy your . . . charms." His insulting gaze traveled her length.

Jennifer drew in her breath sharply. "You can't mean that!" Looking into his implacable face, she faltered. "Kalim, won't you please leave? Tomorrow we—"

"Tomorrow I will have the memory of a night of love," he cut in smoothly. One eyebrow peaked sardonically and his hand stroked the curve of her hip where it was covered by the satin panties. "Tonight I will possess you and I will try to forget the other men who have preceded me."

His fingers made a slow trailing circuit of her satin-clad waist, straying up to fondle the bare skin above the elastic. Jennifer struggled with every ounce of her strength, but his mouth drowned out her cries of protest. Parting her lips forcefully, his mouth ravaged hers with a brutal masculinity.

When she pushed with all her might against his shoulders, Kalim laughed and captured both her hands, holding them behind her back so that she was helpless. In desperation she tried to kick, but her stockinged feet suffered more damage than his hard shins. Finally, she collapsed against him in exhaustion, realizing that her struggles were only inciting him further.

Her surrender produced a change in Kalim. Relaxing his punishing grip, he held her more gently. The hand holding her wrists relaxed its cruel pressure and the other hand massaged the tense muscles at the nape of her neck. Jennifer remained rigid in his arms, trying to show her contempt for his actions, but he didn't release her. Slipping the robe from her taut body, he held her away from him for a moment and looked at her with glowing eyes.

"You are so lovely," he muttered thickly, his hands almost spanning her narrow waist.

Color flooded Jennifer's cheeks as she tried to cover her half-naked body, but he wouldn't permit it. His fingers spread out over her silken skin, sliding up to cup her full breasts, and his avid mouth captured first one and then the other.

The scorching kisses lit a dormant flame and even without the tenderness that had been present the last time Kalim made love to her, Jennifer's treacherous body responded to his passionate touch. She fought against it fiercely, twisting in his arms and uttering a despairing cry, but his insistent mouth stifled her protest.

His deep kiss invaded her very soul and the hands that had been trying to push him away now clutched helplessly at his shoulders. Jennifer felt her willpower slipping away as his hands brought her inflamed body to throbbing, vibrant life.

Trying to remember that he was only trying to

humiliate her was all in vain. A wild yearning for release filled her and she ached to surrender to the untamed desire that made her tremble all over. Winding her arms around his neck, she suddenly gave up the struggle and uttered his name with a low moan.

She was drowning in her love for him, but Kalim's reaction was shocking. Twisting his hand in her hair, he pulled her head back savagely and looked at her with blazing eyes. "Did you call out his name like that, too?" Her drugged eyes looked at him uncomprehendingly as he taunted, "I am surprised you can keep us apart!"

With a look of bitter revulsion, he threw her violently from him and she collapsed on a chair. Slowly sanity returned and she realized that once more he had made her respond to him and then rejected her. Covering her face with her hands, she rested it on her knees and huddled into a miserable little ball.

"What pose is this?" his mocking voice intruded.

"Go away." The plea was muffled. "Just go away and leave me alone." The tears that had threatened for so long finally engulfed her and her slim shoulders shook with the sobs she couldn't stifle.

"What is wrong?" His voice was sharp as he stood looking down. When she didn't answer, he bent down, attempting to raise her head, but she refused to look at him. "Why are you crying?"

The words somehow penetrated her misery and Jennifer felt hysteria bubbling up inside her. Tears had matted her long eyelashes into spiky clusters and her cheeks were flushed with emotion. "I was right about you. You really *are* crazy! Or maybe I'm crazy for letting you get within ten feet of me. Are you proud of yourself? You've just proved one more time that you can make the independent liberated woman melt like hot wax. But that's not much of an accomplishment is it, considering your vast experience and my complete lack of it."

His impassive eyes studied her face. "Do you expect me to believe that after what happened tonight?"

"Would you please tell me what was supposed to have happened tonight?" Frustration flashed like green fire out of her eyes. "Ever since you pushed your way in here, I've had the feeling that I'm in the middle of a nightmare."

"Don't lie to me, Jennifer! I was outside in the hall when John left you."

"So?" She was honestly bewildered.

"He was coming from your bedroom."

A delicate rose stained her cheeks at the implication. "I think you're disgusting to leap to a conclusion like that. This isn't the Victorian era and there are any number of reasons why he could have been coming out of my room. We could have been having a nightcap together, for instance."

"Were you?"

"No, as a matter of fact, we weren't," she said defiantly.

"I am glad you decided not to lie to me anymore. You see, I heard what he said to you—and what you answered."

She searched her mind for anything that could have caused this debacle and came up with a complete blank. "What did he say?"

A spasm of revulsion mixed with pain drew his mouth into a grim line. "I don't remember the exact words, but he said to call him whenever you needed him again and you said . . ." He had trouble continuing. "You said he had been wonderful."

Incredulity widened her eyes. "And you thought . . ." Suddenly anger consumed her and she was so furious she started to shake. "From those few innocent words you jumped to a loathsome conclusion and came charging in here to insult and degrade me!"

He stood up and thrust his hands in his pockets. "They did not sound innocent."

She sprang to her feet also. "I don't have to justify myself to you, but I won't have you spreading vile, unfounded rumors, so I'm going to tell you exactly what went on in this room tonight. John offered to fix my drapes because they wouldn't close properly. Come here." Grabbing his hand, she pulled him across the floor. "See those marks on the carpet? That's where he dragged the table over. Do you want me to stand on it so you can see that I couldn't reach it by myself?"

He stared at her furious face and violent emotions were at war in him. "Is this the truth?"

"Why would I lie?" she cried. "If I wanted to sleep with John or any other man, I would do it and it wouldn't be any of your business. But I don't and I haven't!"

For the first time since she had known him, Kalim seemed uncertain. "When I heard what you said to him . . ."

Jennifer ground her teeth together. "You heard me say, 'You're wonderful. What would I do without you?' Well, I guess it comes down to the old story about people not understanding each other. In my country that's another way of saying, 'Thank you, you did me a big favor.' "

Kalim reached for her, groaning, "Jennifer, what can I possibly say to you? How can I apologize?"

But she backed away. "You can't, and don't touch me! Don't ever touch me again."

He put his arms around her, ignoring her protests. Holding her close in spite of her wild struggles, he stroked her hair gently. "I don't blame you, my darling, but I will make it up to you. It may take the rest of my life"—he kissed the tip of her nose and smiled into her angry eyes—"but that is a possibility devoutly to be desired."

Jennifer's cheek was cradled against his hard shoulder and his caressing hands were beginning to have their familiar effect, but this time she was determined to resist. He would never get another chance to humiliate her, she promised herself fiercely.

"I don't forgive you—not now or ever! I thought for a while that we could be friends, but I see now that even *that* is impossible. We don't understand each other and we have nothing in common."

He kissed the delicate place behind her ear and she raised a shoulder to dislodge his mouth since she couldn't escape from his arms. But his lips strayed across her exposed throat and nibbled at the other ear.

"We have this," he murmured.

She pushed her palms against his chest and looked at him squarely. "I don't like you, Kalim, in spite of the fact that I'll admit I find you physically attractive."

"That is a start." His eyes were filled with merriment as he ignored her anger.

"No, it isn't. We've fought since the moment we met. Why won't you admit we're wrong for each other and stop tormenting me?"

He cupped her chin in his hand and looked at her searchingly. "Have I been doing that?"

"Yes, and I don't understand it! Surely you're not at a loss for female companionship. There are any number of girls who would be delighted to sleep with you." The image of Ayesha surfaced momentarily but she banished it. "Why me?"

"Don't you know?" His eyes devoured her pleading face and she read desire in them . . . and something else. But what?

"No, I don't," she whispered. "I don't know what you want from me."

"I want to take care of you. Yes, I want you for myself, I admit it, but I would be so gentle with you, my darling." His arms folded her close and his words were muffled in her hair as he said savagely, "When I thought you had allowed John to have you, I couldn't stand it. I think I would kill any man who dared to touch you."

The depth of his emotion was unmistakable and Jennifer thought she finally understood. Kalim admitted that he desired her, but he hadn't taken advantage of her innocence. He would have felt guilty for not watching over her more closely if John had seduced her. He meant well—she had to give him that. If only he could have felt something deeper . . .

Jennifer sighed. "I appreciate your concern, Kalim, but you don't have to feel responsible for me. Of course, we both know you engineered this trip, but I'm a grown woman. If I had gotten into any trouble here, it would have been my own fault."

"You think I was concerned because I feel responsible for you?"

Her lashes fell before his molten look. "It's very commendable."

"Jennifer, my darling, sit down." He led her to the couch and sat next to her, still holding her hand. "It is better this way. You are a small scrap of a girl, but no sane man could concentrate with you in his arms." Before continuing, he took out a cigarette and lit it, and the smoke spiraled upward like her heart.

"I do not need to tell you that you are very beautiful. Many men have told you that." His eyes took in the tumbled gilt-colored hair and the jade-green eyes, so bright after their recent tears. "You must know how powerfully you affect me. I have been waiting . . . but perhaps I should ask you now." A slight frown puckered his forehead. Reaching for an ashtray, Kalim abruptly stubbed out his cigarette, and when he turned back to her, he inexplicably changed the subject. "Will you be glad to return to San Francisco?"

"What?" The transition left her with the slightly dazed feeling that a door that had been about to open had been suddenly slammed shut. "Oh . . . yes, I guess . . . I mean, of course I will be."

His face took on a shuttered look. "Yes, of course."

"What was it you wanted to ask me, Kalim?"

"It can wait." He smiled at her. "It is time I left you to your beauty sleep—although no one needs it less."

His knuckle traced the line of her jaw and Jennifer stared at him with parted lips, wanting to know the question he hadn't asked. Something told her it was terribly important to find out now, but as she hesitated, he smoothed her hair gently before turning away. Jennifer followed him to the door, but it was too late—his hand was on the knob and he was halfway into the hall.

"Kalim . . . ?"

Taking her chin in his palm, he smiled warmly at her. Then his mouth covered hers in a kiss that was so sweet that Jennifer's heart swelled with pure love. She put her hands on his shoulders but he reached up and took them in his, saying, "Good night, little dove, sleep well."

Neither of them noticed that the door across the hall was open just a crack. As Jennifer watched Kalim's retreating back, all of her attention was focused on him and conflicting emotions churned inside of her. After a long moment, she sighed and turned away, unaware of Ayesha's smoldering vicious stare.

Chapter Ten

Kalim was gone by the time Jennifer got to his suite the next morning and the turmoil within her was still present. After last night she wouldn't know what to say to him. The first part had been just plain awful, but his explanation and his tender treatment afterward had almost made it worthwhile.

Jennifer's eyes grew dreamy as she remembered the taste of his lips on hers and the gentle stroking of those long, well-shaped fingers. With a shiver of pure bliss, she pushed the memory to the back of her mind and approached the desk.

Today was the end of the conference, so they were pretty well caught up on work, but there were a few things to polish off. She did some typing, put all the reports and press releases in neat piles, and made a series of notes for Kalim, but after everything was done, it was still only early afternoon.

At first she had been buoyed up by a feeling of euphoria, but as the clock ticked away, her spirits gradually sank, realizing her job was over and there would be nothing to keep her here. The time was near when Kalim would be sending her home.

How could she bear not seeing him every day? A

wild hope gripped her when she thought of how he had held her last night, but she knew it was wishful thinking to believe it would make any difference. Oh, he wanted her, all right—that much they shared in common. But she had love to offer and he had only desire.

Jennifer swallowed the lump in her throat and renewed her vow to keep their parting light. She would make it easy for him. There would be no tears or pleas to keep in touch and write to her once in a while. A clean break would be more merciful. But it wouldn't stop her loving him and it wouldn't set her free. She knew with a bittersweet regret that he had destroyed any chance of her ever marrying any other man. Would she ever find anyone worthy to take Kalim's place in her heart or would they all be dwarfed by his giant shadow?

That line of thought was madness. Soon she would be in tears, and what if Kalim came in and caught her crying? How did she propose to explain it this time? Jennifer squared her shoulders determinedly. Taking her cosmetic case out of her purse, she went into the bathroom to freshen up. With a little color on her pale cheeks and after running a comb through her hair, she looked and felt better.

It wasn't necessary to stay cooped up all alone here. The work was finished and the switchboard would take Kalim's calls. Why not look on the positive side of things? There was a big, exciting city out there, and she might as well take advantage of this last chance to see it.

Crossing the bridge that led from the Island of Roda to the city itself, Jennifer looked down at the sparkling Nile and knew she had made the right decision. There was so much she hadn't seen yet.

Her destination was the Alabaster Mosque. Practically modern by Egyptian standards, construction on it was begun in 1830 by Mohammed Ali and completed

more than twenty years later by Said. Jennifer had seen
it from a distance because it dominated the northern
heights of the Citadel, but viewed up close it was
breathtaking. The stately rounded dome and twin
minarets rose majestically above the courtyard and the
huge doors were a masterpiece in themselves.

The interior dwarfed her with its vastness and lofty
vaulted ceilings. Only the hanging crystal globe lights
were a jarring note, their modernity seeming intrusive.
But nothing could really detract from the magnificence
of the alabaster walls from which the mosque drew its
name.

Drifting out to the interior courtyard, Jennifer's eyes
were beguiled by the rhythm of the countless archways
flowing into each other in a soothing unbroken line. In
this symmetrical, ordered world time had no meaning
and she strolled the neat paths lost in visions of the
past.

Thinking she had seen it all but reluctant to leave,
Jennifer wandered around the back, and the sight that
greeted her caused an audible gasp of pleasure. Spread
out before her dazzled eyes was all of Egypt, or so it
seemed. In the distance were the Pyramids of Giza as
well as those of Saqqara and Dahshur. In the opposite
direction the Nile looked like a colored ribbon tying up
skyscrapers, ancient mosques, and modern houses. The
tombs of the Caliphs and Mamelukes were interspersed, waiting in their timeless way for this too to
pass.

She could have stood there for hours drinking in the
beauty and the brooding mystery, but a duskiness in
the sky warned her that it was getting late. Regretfully,
she turned away to look for a taxi, promising herself
that someday she'd return to this magic land.

Jennifer was relaxed and pleasantly tired as she
walked down the corridor of the hotel. She thought of
stopping in Kalim's suite and then decided against it.

She had left him a note, and if he wanted her he would call. Nothing prepared her for the events that were to take place next.

As she approached Kalim's open door, Jennifer heard loud voices, but it meant nothing to her. Only when she recognized one of them as Ayesha's did she react, but she forced herself to keep going. However, Ayesha spied her and came flying out of the room.

Grasping Jennifer's arm with long red fingernails that dug into the flesh, she cried out triumphantly, "Here she is! Here's the little thief!"

Jennifer was sure she hadn't heard correctly. "What did you say?"

Kalim had followed Ayesha into the hall and now he dragged her away and shook her savagely, his face white with rage. "Will you stop making a fool of yourself?"

Her black hair was tumbled in wild disarray, but her glittering eyes regarded him confidently. "You think so, do you? We will soon see who is the fool."

"What's going on?" Jennifer asked helplessly.

The dark girl whirled on her like an avenging angel. "As if you didn't know," she said contemptuously.

"No, I *don't* know—why don't you tell me?" Jennifer's tone was icy. No matter how determined she was not to lose her temper, the other girl always set her teeth on edge.

"Are you trying to deny that you stole my ruby bracelet?"

"What?" Jennifer's gasp was the last of her breath. She felt as though someone had just tossed a medicine ball straight at her midrift.

"Come inside," Kalim commanded, "both of you! We do not need to put on a display for the others on this floor."

Jennifer followed him dumbly, her mind in turmoil.

172

But once inside she turned to Ayesha. "What did you mean?"

"I do not think I have to repeat it," Ayesha sneered. "You stole my bracelet. I saw you coming out of my room and I thought it was strange, but I decided not to say anything because Kalim has a blind spot where you are concerned." She shot him an angry look. "But this is just too much. If you do not return my property this instant, I am going to bring charges." Her eyes narrowed malevolently. "I do not think you would like an Egyptian prison, although it is what you deserve."

"You must be crazy," Jennifer cried. "I was never in your room and I don't know anything about your stupid bracelet."

"Jennifer, let me handle this," Kalim ordered.

"No!" Ayesha flashed. "I will not let you shield this creature. I demand that her room be searched."

"Are you out of your mind?" Kalim's eyes glittered and he restrained himself with an effort, his long fingers closing and unclosing.

"No, she's right." Jennifer's anger was almost as great as his. "I demand that my room be searched. And then *maybe* I'll accept your apology," she said to Ayesha, "but I very much doubt it."

"We will see who apologizes," the other girl said confidently.

"Jennifer, this is not necessary, you do not have to—" Kalim began, but she cut him off in midsentence.

"I *want* you to do it. I've taken a lot from her, but this is the last straw. I'm not going to leave here under a cloud."

"That would not be the case. No one suspects you of anything."

"Speak for yourself, Kalim," Ayesha told him bitterly. "But let us see what you have to say when you are faced with the evidence."

"I will not be a party to anything this vulgar and crude," he lashed out furiously.

"What is the matter?" she taunted. "Are you afraid you may find out your little dove"—the sarcasm was heavy—"is really a vulture after all?"

"Oh, will you two stop all this talking and let's get on with it?" Jennifer cried. "Come with me." And she marched out of the suite.

Ayesha followed her willingly, Kalim reluctantly, and Habeeb brought up the rear. Throughout the noisy scene Habeeb had been a silent spectator, watching and listening. As Kalim's shadow, his presence was so expected that it usually went unnoticed, as it did now.

Jennifer flung open her door and stretched one arm out. "Be my guest," she told Ayesha grimly. When Kalim would have spoken to her, she turned and followed Ayesha into the room. "All right, start searching."

Ayesha stood in the middle of the floor, looking around thoughtfully. "Now where would I hide something if I were a thief?" Jennifer could hear Kalim's heavy breathing, but when she frowned and shook her head, he restrained himself.

"Well, of course, there is always the mattress," Ayesha said. Going over to the bed, she threw the bedspread aside and pulled out the sheets, tossing them in a great tangled mess. Jennifer clenched her fists but managed to remain silent. After sliding her hand an inch or two under the mattress, Ayesha said, "No, I guess that is too unimaginative even for you."

"Well, let's see. There is also the pocket of a dressing gown. Isn't that supposed to be a good hiding place?" She seemed to be enjoying herself, like a little girl playing treasure hunt at a party. Going over to the closet, she regarded its meager contents with a sneer. Then, after pawing carelessly through the lot, she turned back with a perplexed air.

"If you're through making a mess of my things, perhaps you'll leave and let me straighten up," Jennifer said through gritted teeth.

"Oh, I am not through. Whatever gave you that idea? I have not looked in the drawers yet." Jennifer started toward her and then thought better of it as Ayesha sauntered slowly toward the inlaid chest.

She forced herself to watch without protest as Ayesha jumbled her things together contemptuously, but Kalim's patience wasn't as enduring. "This has gone far enough," he stormed. "What do you think you are accomplishing by this charade?"

Ayesha's back was to him but she turned with a smug look on her face. Held between her thumb and forefinger was an exquisite bracelet of glowing rubies interspersed with flashing diamonds. It was obviously worth a fortune. "This is what I have accomplished. Now do you believe me?"

"Where did that come from?" Jennifer gasped.

"As though you did not know." Ayesha's scornful glance scorched her.

"But I didn't . . ." Jennifer turned wildly to Kalim. "I didn't take it, you have to believe me. I never saw it before this minute."

"It will not do you any good to appeal to Kalim. His eyes are opened at last." Ayesha put her hand on his arm and looked up appealingly. "I am sorry I had to do it, beloved, but it was the only way."

Jennifer felt as though she were drowning, but she made an effort to save herself. "Kalim, I know it looks bad, but I swear to you I don't know how that bracelet got in my drawer."

He was looking at Ayesha and it was doubtful that he even heard Jennifer's words. The terrible anger was gone from his eyes to be replaced by an emotion that looked like regret. After studying her triumphant face for a long moment, he said in a low voice, "I am sorry. I never realized."

Jennifer felt a sharp stab of pain in her breast. Hot tears filled her eyes, spilling unheeded down her cheeks at his callous words. He believed that Jennifer was a thief and he was telling Ayesha that he was sorry he never realized it before. Right in front of her! Without even giving her a chance to explain. Well, what did she expect? It was her word against Ayesha's and the evidence was all against her. But he could at least have waited for an explanation instead of turning away without even looking at her.

Jennifer didn't know how the bracelet had gotten into her drawer and at the moment she didn't even care. Kalim was what mattered. He had condemned her without a trial.

Panic rose in her throat as she realized that any second now he would turn on her with those icy cold eyes and flay her with venomous words. That was more than she could bear and Jennifer knew she had to get away before it happened. The tears came faster now, blinding her so that she could barely see the door as she rushed past Habeeb and ran down the hall.

She was still running when she got outside, but a catch in her side made her slow down. Where was she going? Jennifer looked around blankly and realized with a sinking feeling that she didn't know. She had never felt so alone in her life—abandoned in an alien world without a single friend. Then it came to her. John! He would help her. Looking anxiously at her watch, she wondered if he would still be at the museum. He had told her that he often worked late. With a prayer on her lips, she hailed a cab.

For the first time that day luck was with her and John was at the museum. He greeted her warmly and then took a second look. "What's wrong, Jennifer, you look like you've had a shock."

Without any preamble, the words tumbled out of her, but he seemed to have trouble comprehending. "Wait a minute, back up a little. I don't understand this at all."

So she started at the beginning and told him the whole story, concluding, "You see why I have to get away, but I don't have a passport or any money. I thought if you'd go with me to the American Embassy and back up my story they'd believe *you*—you're working with the Egyptian government. The Embassy could fix it up somehow and I'll pay back the money for my ticket." Tears welled up again. "All I want to do is go home."

Jennifer had expected John to react with immediate offers of sympathy and support. When he hesitated, the first fingers of misgiving touched her spine. "This is an amazing story you've just laid on me, Jennifer."

"You do believe me, don't you?"

"Oh, sure—at least . . . I mean, sure."

She looked at him in horror. "You can't believe I stole that bracelet?"

"No, of course not," he assured her, "but the rest of your story—well, it presents problems."

"What do you mean?"

He appeared ill at ease. "I don't think it would do any good to go to the Embassy. They would just tell you to go back to Kalim and ask him for your passport."

"No! I don't ever want to see him again."

"You're being unreasonable, Jennifer. He seemed like a nice guy to me. Don't you think you're blowing this out of all proportion?"

"You didn't hear a word I said, did you?" she whispered.

"About the bracelet, you mean? I wouldn't worry about that. She got it back and I'm sure they'll be happy to hush up the whole incident." Each word struck Jennifer like a blow, but he carefully ignored her stricken face. "All you have to do is remind Kalim that he still has your passport. It probably just slipped his mind."

"I couldn't face him," she breathed. A sudden hope flamed into life. "Would you do it for me, John?"

He avoided meeting her eyes. "You don't need me."

"But I do! He wouldn't dare refuse you. He knows your work here is all tied up with the government."

"But that's just the point, don't you see? Kahira is a very influential man. If he's as furious as you say, he might take out his anger on anyone who . . ." He paused and chose his words with more care. "Kalim has friends in high places—look at the people he was with the night we met him. If he decided to throw his weight around, my whole mission could be down the tube."

She couldn't believe what she was hearing. "You just said he was a nice guy."

"Well, yes, but in a case like this . . . I can't afford to take any chances. You can see my position, can't you?"

"Oh, yes, I can see perfectly," she answered bitterly.

"I'm sure you're making a big deal out of nothing," he assured her. "Why don't you go back to the hotel now and I'll call you later."

The angry words that sprang to Jennifer's lips were never uttered. What was the use? Her shoulders sagged with defeat as she turned and walked out the door.

"I wish you wouldn't look like that, Jennifer. Everything's going to work out fine—you'll see."

The words pelted off her retreating back and echoed eerily in the silent corridor but she barely heard them. John had been her last hope. What was she going to do now?

The darkness outside matched her mood and she welcomed its enveloping cloak. Walking aimlessly down the street, her numbed mind refused to grapple with the problem anymore. She started to count her steps. One, two, three, four—the pointless little game had an hypnotic effect. People passed her on the sidewalk and the headlights of speeding cars briefly illuminated her white face but she was unaware of any of them. Her legs functioned automatically, carrying her down block after block, but she was like a sleep-walker, living in a dream—or a nightmare.

Soon she would wake up in her own bed, Jennifer assured herself. It was very warm for San Francisco though, wasn't it? And the crowds were especially bad. There must be a lot of tourists in town.

A hand on her arm brought her back to reality. "Baksheesh, miss? Something for the poor?" A filthy beggar was leering up at her, his blackened teeth bared in a grin.

Looking around, Jennifer realized with alarm that she was in the native quarter. The narrow darkened streets seemed even more cluttered than before and the swarthy faces surrounding her were unmistakably hostile.

A group of men in long tan robes striped in black were eyeing her boldly, their lascivious eyes roving over her slender figure. Jennifer remembered Kalim's warning and a sudden smothering fear rose in her throat.

When they started toward her, Jennifer looked around wildly for help, but all she saw were beggars with avid eyes. Backing away, she bumped into someone and cried out instinctively as a strong hand fastened around her wrist. She looked over her shoulder and her heart took a lurch. It was Habeeb! Fear turned to terror at this new threat and she tried to twist away, but he held her easily.

Before she could protest, his guttural voice rang out commandingly and the menacing men slunk away into the shadows. Then, still without a word to her, he pulled her toward the curb and hailed a passing taxi.

What did she intend to do with her? Not until they

were safely inside did Jennifer find her voice and then she asked apprehensively, "Where are you taking me?"

"I take you home."

Home? Hysterical laughter rose in her throat but she managed to control it. "Do you mean to the hotel?" He nodded briefly without volunteering any more information. "Did Kalim send you after me? And how did you know where to find me? How did you happen to turn up just when—" She broke off with a shudder.

Habeeb turned opaque black eyes on her and the lights of a passing car illuminated the livid scar on his cheek, but for the first time Jennifer didn't shrink from him. Perhaps there just wasn't any emotion left, but she suddenly realized that she wasn't afraid of Habeeb anymore. He had rescued her from a terrible situation, but she still didn't know how it had come about and he refused to explain.

"The master will tell you when we return."

There was a finality to the words that warned her he wasn't going to say any more no matter how many questions she asked, so Jennifer remained silent. But it didn't stop her mind from spinning. It was obvious that Kalim had sent him. But why? Where could she go without money or a passport? He must have known that she would have to return sooner or later.

Perhaps he couldn't wait to mete out punishment. Would he really turn her over to the police? Jennifer's blood ran cold as she recalled the horrendous things she'd heard about foreign prisons. Surely they would give her a trial! But what would her defense be? Forcing herself to relive every minute of that ghastly search of her room left Jennifer as much in the dark as ever. How could the bracelet have gotten into her drawer? And how could she convince anyone of her innocence without an explanation?

By the time they got to the hotel, Jennifer's nerves were as taut as a rubber band wound around a toy airplane and she was just as ready to fly apart. She was trembling so badly that Habeeb reached out to support her, but she shook off his helping hand. Hesitating at the door a moment, Jennifer took a deep breath and squared her slim shoulders. She wasn't going to be dragged inside like a runaway puppy.

Habeeb opened the door and Jennifer's pulse started to beat like a drum when she saw Kalim savagely pacing the floor. It was going to be even worse than she had feared.

His back was turned but at the sound of the door opening he whirled around and stared at her. A wealth of emotion played over his mobile features and Jennifer braced herself for a tirade that didn't come. Instead Kalim reached out and took her in his arms.

Holding her in a grip so tight that she thought her ribs might crack, he said, "Where have you been? I've been out of my mind with worry!" Having braced herself for something so different, Jennifer couldn't comprehend this reaction. What did it mean? "Don't ever do that to me again," he was murmuring brokenly. "I could not stand it."

With an effort she managed to get enough breath to say, "Wha . . . what are you talking about?"

"Why did you run away like that?" he asked, touching her face as though to reassure himself she was really there.

Pain darkened her eyes. "Don't play with me, Kalim. You know why. You believed Ayesha's story. You didn't even ask me if I took the bracelet."

"Is that what you thought?" Incredulity colored his voice.

A great sadness filled her. "I don't know how it got in my drawer. I guess it's too much to expect you to believe me, but you could at least have asked."

"Oh, my darling—I didn't have to ask. I knew you didn't take that wretched bracelet."

181

"But you said . . . you didn't even look at me. You said . . ." Jennifer choked up and couldn't continue.

He took her chin in his hand and looked at her lovingly. "What did I say?"

"You told Ayesha you hadn't realized before that I was a thief."

With a gentle forefinger he wiped away the tears that were gathering on her long eyelashes. "That is not what I said."

"Well, maybe those weren't the exact words but—"

"My poor baby, never did I mean to imply such a thing. No, actually, I was voicing my thoughts aloud. Come, sit down and I will explain." In a daze, Jennifer allowed herself to be led to the couch. Then, with his arm around her, Kalim continued. "When Ayesha was growing up, I was aware of the fact that she had what you would call a crush on me. It was harmless enough and I was amused by it. As she became older there were swarms of young men attracted to her and I naturally assumed that she had outgrown her schoolgirl infatuation. I regarded her as a little sister and I thought she looked upon me as her big brother. It was not until tonight in your room that I realized my mistake."

"I could have told you that a long time ago," Jennifer muttered resentfully.

Kalim grinned. "I plead guilty." His smile faded as he said, "I not only failed to see that she was in love with me, I did not realize how far she would go to keep us apart. She could tell that I loved you deeply. Why did you not know it, my darling?"

Jennifer's heart started to beat wildly and she looked at him with uncertain eyes. "Kalim, I—"

But he interrupted. "Never mind. We will get to that in a moment. First we must finish the odious subject of the bracelet. I never suspected you for an instant. Even before Habeeb told me the truth of the matter."

"Habeeb? What has he to do with this?"

"He saw Ayesha going into your room after you had left the hotel this afternoon. He was going to tell me about it but the occasion did not arise until after she had made her accusation."

"She went into my—then she must have put the bracelet there herself!" The explanation was so simple it was almost laughable except that this had been no laughing matter. But it was all over now and Jennifer felt almost giddy with relief. Impulsively, she threw her arms around Kalim's neck. "You don't know what this means to me!"

He gathered her close and she could hear the steady thud of his heart against hers. "And *you* do not know what it means to have you back safely. I almost went out of my head with worry, imagining you alone out there in the darkness. When I think what could have happened to you . . ."

If he only knew! Jennifer shivered involuntarily and glanced at Habeeb. He gave a barely perceptible shake of his head and she knew they had just entered into a conspiracy to protect Kalim's peace of mind.

"But how did he find me?" The question was directed as much to Habeeb as Kalim.

"I can only guess." Kalim looked inquiringly at the big man. "You followed her when she ran out?" Habeeb nodded.

"But I never saw him," she cried.

"You would not if he did not wish it." Remembering how silently the huge man could move, Jennifer nodded her head, and Kalim said, "He is a man of many talents, the greatest being devotion. Habeeb takes care of his loved ones."

It sounded like he was saying—but Jennifer was afraid to believe what her ears were telling her so she chose her words with great care. "Yes, you once told me that he would do anything for you."

"I do not think he did this only for me," Kalim said, smiling.

Jennifer looked at Habeeb and for the first time saw his ugly face split into a huge grin. The transformation was startling, and looking into his steady eyes, Jennifer realized that she had been accepted and would have a friend for life.

"Thank you, Habeeb," she whispered. Inclining his head, he acknowledged her thanks and left her alone with Kalim.

"And now that we are finished with that, it is time to get to important matters," Kalim said. "My work here is finished and it is time to leave." He hesitated for a second. "There is something I must ask you. Do you still resent me because I tricked you into coming here?"

"Oh, no, Kalim! It's been an experience I wouldn't have missed for anything. I know I . . . I acted abominably in the beginning, but—"

"Hush, my darling." He silenced her with a kiss, which she returned eagerly, wrapping her arms tightly around his neck. The gentle pressure of his lips increased at her willing response and his mouth bored down on hers, possessing her with mounting passion. His arms strained her so close that they were almost like one person and Jennifer's surrender was complete.

Her throbbing desire rose to meet his, but with a great effort Kalim reached up and unclasped her arms. Moving away, he lit a cigarette with shaking fingers. "If we continue in this way I will find it impossible to say what must be said."

Jennifer could scarcely believe it. It was almost exactly like that night he had been about to make love to her. She had practically thrown herself at him then and he had rejected her. And now he was doing it again. When would she ever learn? In an agony of pain, she said stiffly, "You don't have to put it into words. I understand."

"You do?"

"Yes, you're sending me home." A sad little lopsided smile tried to establish itself. "Well, don't worry—I'll have only nice things to say about you."

He looked at her with a mixture of disbelief, annoyance, and tenderness. "Jennifer, what am I going to do with you? You make it very difficult for a man to ask you to marry him." Despair was suddenly replaced by a wild hope that made her heart sing as he said, "I was going to wait until I returned you to your own country, but I dare not wait any longer. You misunderstand my every action. Will you marry me, Jennifer?"

It was the fulfillment of all her dreams and she cried, "Oh, yes, Kalim! Yes, I will! Why did you wait so long?"

He took her gently in his arms and tenderly stroked her hair. "In the beginning you did not trust me and when I forced you to come here I was afraid you hated me."

"No, no, never," she cried.

He put one finger on her lips and kissed the tip of her nose. "Then when I realized you were beginning to return my love, I thought it best to wait until you were back in familiar surroundings. You were so alone and vulnerable here. I wanted you to be sure of your answer."

Jennifer was overwhelmed by the depth of his feeling and her heart sang a love song to this wonderful man. Only one small thing clouded her bliss. She touched the curly black hair on his bronzed chest where it was revealed by the open neck of his silk shirt. Why bring it up now? But it was something she had to know.

A rosy pink flooded her cheeks as she raised her head. "Kalim, there is something I want to ask you."

"Yes, my darling?"

"That night . . . when Ayesha came to the door. You told her you were *glad* she had come."

185

The effort was too great and she bowed her head, but he put his hand under her chin and raised it, forcing her to look at him. "Never be shy with me, little dove. Yes, I was glad she interrupted us at that moment. I wanted you then and I want you now, but not like that. I want you to be my wife." His eyes gleamed with sudden merriment. "My one and only wife forever and always."

Silhouette Romance

IT'S YOUR OWN SPECIAL TIME

Contemporary romances for today's women.
Each month, six very special love stories will be yours
from SILHOUETTE. Look for them wherever books are sold
or order now from the coupon below.

$1.50 each

Hampson	☐ 1	☐ 4	☐ 16	☐ 27	Browning	☐ 12	☐ 38	☐ 53	☐ 73
	☐ 28	☐ 52	☐ 94			☐ 93			
Stanford	☐ 6	☐ 25	☐ 35	☐ 46	Michaels	☐ 15	☐ 32	☐ 61	☐ 87
	☐ 58	☐ 88			John	☐ 17	☐ 34	☐ 57	☐ 85
Hastings	☐ 13	☐ 26			Beckman	☐ 8	☐ 37	☐ 54	☐ 96
Vitek	☐ 33	☐ 47	☐ 84		Wisdom	☐ 49	☐ 95		
Wildman	☐ 29	☐ 48			Halston	☐ 62	☐ 83		

☐ 5 Goforth	☐ 22 Stephens	☐ 50 Scott
☐ 7 Lewis	☐ 23 Edwards	☐ 55 Ladame
☐ 9 Wilson	☐ 24 Healy	☐ 56 Trent
☐ 10 Caine	☐ 30 Dixon	☐ 59 Vernon
☐ 11 Vernon	☐ 31 Halldorson	☐ 60 Hill
☐ 14 Oliver	☐ 36 McKay	☐ 63 Brent
☐ 19 Thornton	☐ 39 Sinclair	☐ 71 Ripy
☐ 20 Fulford	☐ 43 Robb	☐ 76 Hardy
☐ 21 Richards	☐ 45 Carroll	☐ 78 Oliver

☐ 81 Roberts
☐ 82 Dailey
☐ 86 Adams
☐ 89 James
☐ 90 Major
☐ 92 McKay
☐ 97 Clay
☐ 98 St. George
☐ 99 Camp

$1.75 each

Stanford	☐ 100	☐ 112	☐ 131	Hampson	☐ 108	☐ 119	☐ 128	☐ 136
Hardy	☐ 101	☐ 130			☐ 147	☐ 151	☐ 155	☐ 160
Cork	☐ 103	☐ 148		Browning	☐ 113	☐ 142	☐ 164	
Vitek	☐ 104	☐ 139	☐ 157	Michaels	☐ 114	☐ 146		
Dailey	☐ 106	☐ 118	☐ 153	Beckman	☐ 124	☐ 154		
Bright	☐ 107	☐ 125		Roberts	☐ 127	☐ 143	☐ 163	
				Trent	☐ 110	☐ 161		

CITY

$1.75 each

Silhouette Desire
15-Day Trial Offer

A new romance series
that explores
contemporary relationships
in exciting detail

Six Silhouette Desire romances, free for 15 days!
We'll send you six new Silhouette Desire romances
to look over for 15 days, absolutely free! If you decide
not to keep the books, return them and owe nothing.

Six books a month, free home delivery. If you like
Silhouette Desire romances as much as we think you
will, keep them and return your payment with the
invoice. Then we will send you six new books every
month to preview, just as soon as they are published.
You pay only for the books you decide to keep, and
you never pay postage and handling.

Coming next month from
Silhouette Romances

The Tender Years by Anne Hampson

As Christine changed into a woman her feelings toward Luke
Curtis changed as well. He was no longer her childhood mentor.
Something more was growing between them—something that
would alter Christine's life forever.

Mermaid's Touch by Patti Beckman

In her underwater world no problems existed for Amy Peterson.
But once she emerged from the Aquarena her problems crashed
down around her. Would a no-love merger with Scott Creighton
be her only way out?

Island Of Flowers by Nora Roberts

When Laine came to Hawaii to make amends with her father his
young business partner tried to thwart the reconciliation. She
realized that Dillion must overcome his mistrust of her; for only
then would she find his love.

Man Of Velvet by Dana Terrill

Caleb blamed Dianna for Barrett's death and wanted to avenge
Barrett through his own loveless marriage to Dianna. Dianna
couldn't imagine anything worse—until she found herself falling
in love with the man who hated her.

Sweet Eternity by Rita Clay

Brenna had a choice: security, or love with a man who would
always be between tournaments—and women. Could she resist
his pressure? But then did she really want to?

No Trifling With Love by Mary Lee Stanley

When Connie took a teaching job she hoped her afternoon with
the mysterious George Trevelyan would fade from her mind. But
her heart told her he was not the type to be easily forgotten.

READERS' COMMENTS ON SILHOUETTE ROMANCES:

"I would like to congratulate you on the most wonderful books I've had the pleasure of reading. They are a tremendous joy to those of us who have yet to meet the man of our dreams. From reading your books I quite truly believe that he will some-day appear before me like a prince!"

—L.L.*, Hollandale, MS

"Your books are great, wholesome fiction, always with an upbeat, happy ending. Thank you."

—M.D., Massena, NY

"My boyfriend always teases me about Silhouette Books. He asks me, how's my love life and natu-rally I say terrific, but I tell him that there is always room for a little more romance from Sil-houette."

—F.N., Ontario, Canada

"I would like to sincerely express my gratitude to you and your staff for bringing the pleasure of your publications to my attention. Your books are well written, mature and very contemporary."

—D.D., Staten Island, NY

*names available on request